SILVER RIVER SHADOW

JANE THOMAS
WITH
ROCHELLE LAMM

BOOKS & BICYCLES

First published in UK, US and Canada in August 2022 by
Books & Bicycles Press
Print Edition

www.booksandbicycles.com

Text copyright © Jane Thomas 2022
www.jane-thomas.co.uk
Illustration copyright © Sarah Jane Docker 2022
www.sarahjanedocker.com

The moral rights of the author and illustrator have been
asserted

Produced in conjunction with the Mercury Tragedy Project

Paperback ISBN 978 1 8381813 3 8
Ebook ISBN 978 1 8381813 4 5

To the adventurer inside us all

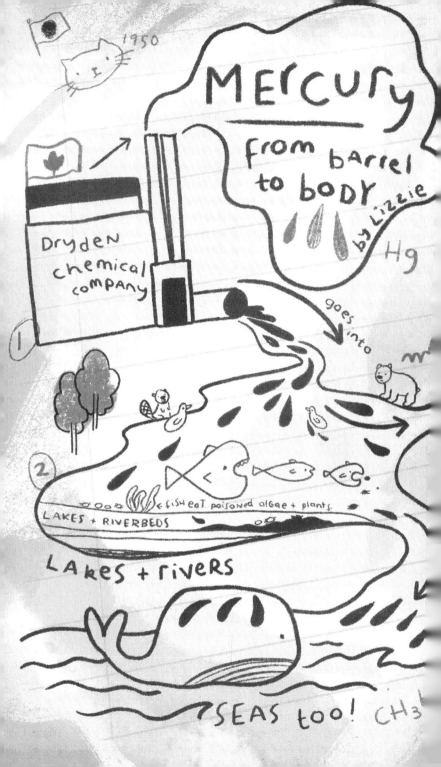

November 1865, Oxford, England

Charles Dodgson, later known as Lewis Carroll, sits down to write a story for his friend's niece. He includes a character who becomes popularly known as 'The Mad Hatter'.

June 1950, Minamata, Japan

A little girl sits and watches as a cat with terror-filled eyes runs round and round in a circle, catching her breath as the creature suddenly stops circling and drops to the ground.

CHAPTER 1

THE BEGINNING OF THE END

September 15th, 2021

Lizzie stared out of the classroom window, beyond the playground and up towards the clouds. Perhaps if she wished hard enough they'd get grayer and heavier. Perhaps if she really wanted it to happen, the clouds would club together and form a storm. And somehow that storm might be so awful that it would send bolts of lightning directly onto the school. Maybe one would even set fire to it – no, wait, scratch that, she didn't want anyone to be hurt.

She just really, really didn't want to give her presentation.

It wasn't that she had nothing to say. Lizzie tuned back in to Mary-Anne's speech, a list punctuated regularly by 'and then'. Mary-Anne stared at her paper and didn't dare look above it, at her classmates, which was probably as well since they were all engaged in napping or passing notes or, like Lizzie, staring wistfully at the outside world. Even Miss Andrews looked as if she was clamping her mouth shut against a yawn.

Lizzie would like to bet Miss Andrews was already regretting the summer assignment. She'd always just told them to write a book report during the holidays, and much as some of those were very dull indeed to listen to at least they included magic or fighting dragons or searching for hidden treasure.

"Tell me about your family!" Miss Andrews had said enthusiastically on the last day of school. "Every family has a story to tell. I want to hear yours!"

So far, it turned out nobody had a story to tell at all. The shops in the small, dusty town had been handed down through the generations; the most exciting anecdotes were about when they'd run out of potatoes one winter (or for three days, at least).

The clock ticked loudly. Mary-Anne had stopped and was awkwardly shuffling her papers at the front of the class. Miss Andrews stood up with a too-wide smile and clapped loudly, nodding towards the students to do the same. So everyone joined in, clapping politely, and those who had been dozing on their desks jerked upright and did some extremely enthusiastic clapping in a bid to make up for their absence.

"Who do we have next?" Miss Andrews asked brightly, running her finger down the list. "Aaron? It looks like it's time to hear all about your family!"

Aaron did his best to pretend he hadn't heard but Mary-Anne whacked him on the head with her papers as she sat down. "You're up," she told him.

He went to the front, turned to face the class, and picked a spot high up on the back wall. For the next quarter of an hour, his gaze would bounce between his notes and that spot, never acknowledging the audience.

"My grandmother came to Littleton in 1964. And then she met my grandfather. And then they were married…".

Lizzie looked back towards the playing field and inwardly screamed "and then" over and over until it became even more meaningless than it already was in the mouths of her classmates. She pulled the carved wooden eagle from her pocket and propped it up on her desk and Bobby, her friend – her only friend – gave her a thumbs up from the far side of the room.

3

He grinned at her and mouthed, 'I can't wait!' before pointing at stammering, monotone Aaron and dramatically crashing back in his chair as if he had quite literally died of boredom.

She pretended to stifle a laugh, although it hadn't been that funny and was really more than a bit mean. It was hardly Aaron's fault the most exciting thing in his family's history was that they'd invented the 'cronut' long before it took off in New York. It's all well and good coming up with ideas, but if you don't tell the rest of the world it's very hard for anyone to give you credit for it.

"A portmanteau," Dad had told her. "When you get two words and mash them together, it's called a portmanteau. Put together 'hungry' and 'angry'. You get 'hangry'."

Thinking of it now, she looked across at Bobby again. And there he was, reaching under his desk to peel back the lid of his lunchbox just far enough that he could slide a few bites of a sandwich into his mouth. That boy was always eating, or thinking about eating, and when he'd been without food for more than an hour... Wow, could he get angry. She wondered how he even made it through the night.

She heard a distant droning sound outside and

4

looked out – out across the playground, out across the trees, and out towards the farthest corners of the horizon, and there in the sky was the Piper Cub. It had to be. Bright yellow, wings stretched out, little wheels reaching down and ready for action. Others heard it, too, and started openly gawping at the tiny plane as it grew larger and larger in the sky, its growing shadow reaching across the field.

Miss Andrews snapped out of her reverie, was about to admonish the children for not even pretending to listen to Aaron, and then caught sight of the plane too.

They all rushed to the windows to get the best view of the plane that was clearly lining up to land along the playground. They shouted and pointed, and Aaron quietly announced, 'The end' in the midst of the chaos and joined them all, very glad indeed to have an excuse to get out of the spotlight.

"Dad," said Lizzie quietly.

"It's your Dad?" said Mary-Anne, and everyone turned to look at Lizzie who went bright red and tried to somehow combine staring at the ground and keeping an eye on the plane.

"Um, yeah. It's Dad. He said he'd come for my presentation so… I guess he came."

"In a crazy little plane?"

"It's not crazy. It's a Piper Cub."

"And I've been in it!" said Bobby.

Everyone swung their eyes from Lizzie to Bobby.

"Oh yes," he said airily. "A few times. It's kind of cool. It lands on water, too. When the pontoons are used, of course."

He walked across to Lizzie and smiled at her.

"You just wait till you hear her story," he told the class.

It's hard to say whether they were more surprised by the presence of the plane, the fact that 'coolest kid in the school' Bobby was talking to 'stuck up' Lizzie, or that she had any story at all. But someone opened the fire exit and they all charged outside just as the plane came to a bouncing halt by the long jump pits, so nobody had to decide what was more surprising after all. Miss Andrews tottered after them in her heels, torn between shouting at them to come back inside and wanting to see the plane herself.

Then there he was, Lizzie's dad, striding towards the teacher with his hand outstretched and an apologetic lopsided smile on his face.

"I'm terribly sorry, Miss," he shrugged, spreading his hands wide. "But I did promise Lizzie I wouldn't

6

miss her presentation, and I didn't want to be late."

"That's quite alright," she stammered. Her Teacher Training hadn't covered Random Arrivals By Plane and she was really rather flustered, patting her hair carefully into place and privately wishing she'd re-done her make-up at lunchtime.

She turned to Lizzie, looking her up and down curiously. "Well, then, I suppose we should find out what's so very special about your presentation." She clapped her hands and started to lead the class back inside but Lizzie interrupted her.

"Miss Andrews? Do you think I might do it outside? Under the big oak tree? Please?"

Miss Andrews looked as though she was about to squash that idea but an entire class of children begging, "Please? Oh, please Miss?" is terribly hard to ignore.

And so they went and gathered their jackets and laid them on the grass in a wide circle, and Bobby carried out a chair for Lizzie to sit on and handed her the little wooden eagle that she had forgotten on her desk, and grinned at his friend.

He spoke to the class as he walked over to his jacket and sat down.

"You just wait, guys. You just wait…".

CHAPTER 2

INTRODUCING THE ATTIC

Three months earlier

Lizzie was one of the last to get off the school bus. She wished, as she always did, that she had somebody to turn around and give a wave goodbye, to call out "Have a great holiday!" to and get back a, "See you tomorrow for swimming!"

But there was none of that for Lizzie. Just a long walk up a dusty road with nothing but the crickets for company. Dad's car wasn't in the driveway when she got home. Of course it wouldn't be, it never was these days. She walked into the kitchen and Mrs. Dabble handed over a smile and an enormous slice of cherry cake.

"Well done! Another school year survived! You excited for the holidays?" she asked, overly bright and breezy.

Lizzie rolled her eyes, regretted the rudeness, and smiled and shrugged through a mouthful of cake.

"I'll be here every day, don't you worry," said Mrs. Dabble. "And your father said you're to eat dinner with him this evening."

Lizzie sighed. That meant he wanted A Talk, and she wasn't sure she was in the mood for A Talk. A Talk more often than not meant a fumbling discussion that he'd decided it was his duty to have about how she felt about her mother (it was hard to feel anything other than an indefinable, inexpressible loss for the mother who had died a few days after she had been born), or how school was going (fine, she did enough work to do well but not enough to stick out), or whether she'd made any friends yet (of course not).

She spent the afternoon rearranging her books. She'd overheard one of the girls at school saying that she'd put hers so they looked like a rainbow, and Lizzie wanted to try that. It was all very well, though, having a rainbow of books, but she quickly realized she'd never find anything again. Sighing, she took them all off the shelf once more and put them sensibly in alphabetical order. That wouldn't do, either, as it seemed so incredibly staid. So she divided them into groups: 'Books I haven't read yet,' 'Books I've read more than once,' 'Books that I will, let's face it, never read'. Then she arranged them on the shelves with some lying sideways and some upright, and snuck little ornaments in between some to break up the line of books.

"You look great," she informed the shelves once she'd finished.

But she did wonder why she'd bothered since nobody but Mrs. Dabble and herself ever saw the shelves.

Staring at the ceiling fan ticking its way through the hot air passed the time well enough until she went down for dinner. The dining room, of course, with Dad at one end of the long table and Lizzie at the other, the salt and pepper shakers a little bit lost in the middle alongside a bunch of flowers Mrs. Dabble had placed there in a desperate bid to make the dark room slightly less overbearing.

They just meant Lizzie and her father could barely see each other.

There was an awkward clattering of knives and forks against ceramic plates, a 'whoops!' from Lizzie as some peas scuttled off her fork and bounced down to the floor, and the slow tick, tock of the grandfather clock that watched over the scene from the corner of the room.

"So how's school?"

"Great, Dad."

She tried to bring some enthusiasm to her answer, hoping he'd go quiet again. But no, he was determined to have a conversation.

"Got any homework for the summer?"

Lizzie swallowed, and dug her nails into her palm.

"We have to write about our family."

She said it bluntly. His fork stopped on the way to his mouth. He studied his plate intently. Lizzie felt her heartbeat was surely louder than the clock's ticking.

The silence extended. It was excruciating. Mrs. Dabble shuffled in and retrieved the plates, came back and replaced them with bowls of fruit salad.

"Er, Mrs. Dabble…".

"Yes, Sir?"

"What's this?"

"It's fruit salad. I think you should both eat more healthily, Sir. Just a thought. Bit of pineapple in there, I was lucky to get that. And I found strawberries growing in the garden. I'm sure you'll like it."

She caught Lizzie's eye as she left and held a

finger to her lips. The cake was their secret.

"Look," he said at last. "There's some boxes of stuff up in the attic. They were your mother's. I think it's things she got from her grandparents. I… I didn't think it was ever my business to poke around in them, but I guess you might as well. It's your family, after all."

How had Lizzie made it to twelve years old and she'd never heard of these boxes? She was about to thank him but he went on.

"I've got a big case on right now. Won't have time to help or anything. I'm sure Mrs. Dabble will be useful."

He got up and was about to leave the room then thought better of it, walked back to Lizzie, and bent over and gave her a kiss on the forehead.

"My little Busy Lizzie…" he said softly, then turned abruptly and headed for his office. The door was closed before she drew breath again.

She toyed with the idea of going to the attic right away, but then the thought of those endless weeks of holiday stretched before her and she decided to take her time. Tomorrow would be fine.

That night, Lizzie dreamed of her mother. It was the same dream she'd had a few times before. Her mother would be standing on the other side of a river, waving to her. Lizzie would look at the river, at how it rushed around jagged rocks, and want to try to cross it but she didn't dare. Her mother would stand on the far side, waving, with that same smile she had in the photograph Lizzie wore in the locket by her heart.

CHAPTER 3

FINDING FRIENDSHIP

Lizzie managed to fill four days before heading into the attic. She picked strawberries and helped Mrs. Dabble with the housework; she read books and thought about daring to turn up at the local swimming spot but in the end she settled for a hose in the garden. As ever, it struck her that life would be significantly improved if she had someone to play with, and she wondered about starting up her 'Let's get a dog' campaign with her father again. But he was hardly around, and if he was then he disappeared into his study.

She went in there one day while he was out. She looked over at the huge whiteboard that hung on an easel. It was covered in comments and arrows that linked and looped, photos stuck on with tape, a map in the corner covered with lines of red strings wrapped around pins that linked places together. The desk was a maze of sticky paper notes. Books balanced precariously in piles and she accidentally knocked over one teetering tower. Stacking them back together, she noticed little tabs sticking out from some of the pages – markers and reminders. Some had notes scribbled in the margin and others were made into rainbows by the sweeps of highlighter pens.

A photo in a silver frame stood on the mantelpiece, her mother calmly watching over this organized chaos. It was the same photo in the locket Lizzie wore around her neck – a smile that promised something wonderful was about to happen, eyes that laughed back at you. Dad had told her he'd taken the photo: it was in front of the Lincoln Memorial, but nobody would know that. He only had eyes for her; nothing else appeared in the shot. Lizzie always thought he must have said something very funny just before he clicked the camera.

"We were together. That's how she always was," he'd told her. And he'd disappeared into his memories that Lizzie didn't want to disturb.

Newspaper clippings were piled onto the desk, most of them accompanied by the same staring face of a woman identified as Irene Ward. The headlines boldly announced hints of the crime, luring in shocked readers, and Lizzie dropped the papers as if they were on fire, running out of the study and slamming the door shut behind her to keep all that horror trapped in its four walls.

There was nothing left to do. The day threatened to stretch into an impossible eternity. It was time to investigate the boxes.

Lizzie would go into the attic twice a year: once to help Dad get the Christmas decorations down, and once to put them back up again. It was full of cobwebs and strange smells, and the sunlight filtered through a single grubby pane. The glow from the lightbulb didn't reach into the corners, the places where she always imagined monsters waiting to reach out and grab her ankles.

Lizzie sat near the open hatch for a while letting her eyes adjust to the gloom. Piles of suitcases sat alongside pictures lined up in rows. An alarming creature with many heads turned out to be a bag of golf clubs. Dusty shoes lay in a jumbled pile.

And countless boxes. So many boxes! Scrawled on the outside of each was a clue to what lay within: "Edward – university." "Rachel – dancing." At the sight of her mother's name, she reached to her locket and pressed it gently to her heart.

Lizzie poked her head into a few of the boxes but it was hard to find any meaning in somebody else's belongings, somebody else's saved treasures.

Two of the boxes didn't have the name of a person. In faded ink, she read: "Ball Lake Lodge". Underneath, someone had carefully added "The Mercury Files". Mercury – the planet? The metal? Something else? Curious, Lizzie pulled out what looked to be an old poster. It was damaged, torn at the corners and terribly faded, but she could make out the words 'Fish for fun' along the top and 'warning' and 'mercury' further down.

She hauled out a pile of papers and moved over to the window. It took all her strength but the catch finally gave and she was able to push it open, fresh air racing in to replace the stagnant, dust dancing in the sunbeams that now threw themselves into the attic. Lizzie went through the pages quickly, trying to get an idea of what she'd found. There were things that looked like the court documents Dad sometimes left lying around. Old newspaper clippings. Magazine articles. A diary. Photographs of a man with a broad smile and a cigar stuck in his mouth, standing next to a seaplane. There were even flight tickets and luggage tags: someone had gone all the way to Japan.

Two names and one theme kept recurring: Barney and Marion Lamm, and mercury. There were graphs and charts with numbers that made no sense to her, talking about mercury levels. Lists of symptoms. Somewhere called 'Grassy Narrows' kept coming up, and 'Whitedog' was everywhere too.

It was no use, she couldn't figure out what was going on or who these people were, or why on earth the boxes were in the attic. She was at the point of heading back downstairs – Mrs. Dabble's cake was waiting to be eaten, after all – when another photo slipped out from between some pages.

Staring back at her was her mother – only it couldn't be her mother, because this photograph was too old and the hair was different somehow, pulled up in a way she'd never seen in any of the pictures of her mother. Turning it over, she read 'Marion, summer 1965, Ball Lake'. Looking at the front again, there was no mistaking the connection between her mother and the mystery Marion. And Lizzie knew that she was turning out just the same; Dad caught his breath sometimes and she'd seen him close his eyes and whisper 'Rachel'.

Marion must be her grandmother – no, with that

date she must be her great-grandmother. Another photograph showed Marion having just married Barney. There they stood, Barney in a suit that looked a little too large, with a stance that announced he was ready to take on the world. Marion looked quieter, a little shy perhaps, but her chin was up and she held a steady gaze.

Lizzie looked back at the boxes, at the chaos she had already created, and she knew this wouldn't work at all. She thought back to Dad's office: his whiteboard, his notes, his arrows. If she was going to make any sense of what was here, she needed supplies.

Armed with a list that started with 'highlighters' and ended with 'chocolate', she shouted a goodbye to Mrs. Dabble, climbed onto her bike and set off for town.

Bobby Bingle was bored. He'd been throwing stones at tin cans for the best part of an hour now and he was already, just four days into the holiday, starting to regret announcing to his parents that he was refusing to go to summer camp this year.

"Fine," they'd said. "You can help on the farm.

You're old enough now," secretly relieved they didn't need to pay for all three boys to go.

And just like that, they'd packed off his two brothers to camp and told him he was 'free to do what he wanted'. Which had been amazing for two days, deliberately staying in bed as long as possible just to wind his dad up, who had shouted something about 'milking' and 'lazy' before stomping out to deal with the cows.

Bobby climbed down off the wall and walked slowly over to the cans, standing them upright once more and gathering a handful of stones.

And in the distance, coming down the dead centre of the long dusty road, someone was riding a bike. Bobby sat and waited as the figure slowly approached and he realized it was Lizzie, the girl with the curly hair who wore strange, ill-fitting clothes, and who sat to the side in class and didn't dare look at anyone.

As she came closer, he rolled the little stones around in his hand. Did he dare…?

"Oh, why not?" he told himself, took aim, and threw one at the front wheel. It pinged off a spoke with a satisfying sound, so he threw another.

Ping!

Bang on target again.

Lizzie just looked across at him, shook her head a little, and carried on riding as if nothing was happening. Her lack of response caught him so off-guard that Bobby was left holding a stone between thumb and forefinger, ready for throwing, when he realized she'd gone too far and he'd missed his chance.

She forced herself to breathe slowly, keeping her gaze ahead and blinking away tears. Bobby Bingle, she told herself, could go boil his head.

There was one store in town that would have what she needed. Town, bear in mind, consisted of one post office (open three mornings a week), Lillian's Cafe (breakfast and lunch, always featuring pancakes and pie), a small supermarket that sold a lot of stuff in packets and not much else, a gas station, and the hardware store. The hardware store is where you went for everything from a balloon to a wardrobe. It was run by an ancient, beach-ball shaped couple who insisted on fetching things themselves, tottering behind the long counters and daring to ease them-selves up ladders to reach the highest shelves.

They fetched her highlighters, sticky notes, a box of chalk and a magnifying glass (Lizzie was taking no chances and besides, all detectives she'd read about had magnifying glasses) and she slipped them into her backpack. Time to head home, and time to head past Bobby Bingle again.

As she came to the turning in the road to go past him, she summoned up all the determination and speed she could muster, pedaling as hard as she could to get past him in – she hoped – the blink of an eye. But as she approached the farm, Bobby leapt off the wall and came rushing out into the road, waving his arms.

"Stop!" He shouted. "Hey, Lizzie, stop!"

It would have been easy to race right round him and leave him standing there but instead she skidded to a halt, looked him levelly in the eyes and simply said, "What?"

"So, look. I'm sorry."

Bobby went bright red. Lizzie stayed silent.

"I mean, I shouldn't have done that. I'm just bored. Aren't you bored? This holiday is taking forever. It's only day four and I'm bored out of my mind. What are you going to do all holiday? Are you going anywhere? I'm staying here. Just me on the farm. My brothers have gone to summer camp. I didn't want to go but now I'm...".

He finally trailed off and laughed awkwardly.

"So… you're bored," she said.

"I guess."

Lizzie gathered up all her courage to extend the conversation. It felt like it was her turn to say something.

"Me too."

Silence. Neither of them knew what to say now.

"So what were you doing in town?"

Lizzie hesitated for a moment. Did she want to share her find with Bobby?

"Just, you know, getting some stuff. I got chocolate. Want some?"

They sat on the wall together and threw stones at the cans. Bobby was secretly impressed with Lizzie's throwing abilities: she could knock three cans down with three stones thrown in quick succession. When he went to put them upright, he moved them further away each time, but Lizzie kept hitting that bullseye. Bobby needed to do something to impress her.

"Do you like canoeing?" he asked casually.

"Yes! No. I mean… I don't know. I've never really, you know, tried it."

It was a hot day – so hot even the flies had given up buzzing and taken up residence in the shade. Being by water seemed like a good idea. She followed

Bobby across a field and down to a small lake, where a long open canoe sat waiting on a towel-sized beach.

"You get in first," instructed Bobby as he handed her a paddle. "I'll push off and leap in behind."

Lizzie remembered the stones thrown at her bike and hesitated. "Promise you'll get in?"

"Scout's honor. Cross my heart and hope to die."

She sat on the little wooden seat at the front of the canoe and clutched her paddle. The boat started to wobble as he pushed it off the beach and she braced her legs against the sides, determined not to let him know she was scared. A bigger wobble as he gave a final push and jumped in behind her then the canoe settled as he slowly paddled it forwards, two long, easy strokes on either side as he confidently maneuvered them around the reeds.

Lizzie looked down and watched the lily pads glide past, some dotted with bright dashes of turquoise dragonflies. Minnows raced away from the canoe, and two turtles sunned themselves on a tiny island.

Bobby watched her watching the lake. He saw her grip on the paddle loosen as the nerves left her, saw her quick private smiles and wide eyes when she turned from one side to the other. Maybe, he thought, maybe the summer holidays wouldn't be so awful after all.

He showed her how to hold the paddle, one hand on top pushing deep into the water, the other hand pulling it back in a strong, smooth motion. She picked it up quickly, learning to push her legs against the sides and use her whole body to haul the paddle back. It was only when they finally returned to shore, a little breathless from racing around the lake, that she realized her hands were covered in blisters.

"You get used to it," he said, showing her his hands with great callouses rising from roughened, toughened skin. "Best thing is just to keep paddling. Work through it."

Lizzie prodded a blister doubtfully.

"Come back tomorrow," Bobby said. "I promise, by the end of a week your hands will be fine."

"I'd like that," she said shyly. "I have to do this project first –". She stopped herself. She hadn't meant to mention that. Not yet.

"What project? Oh, the 'tell the story of your family' thing? Mine's easy. 'Great-great grandfather was a farmer. Great-grandfather was a farmer. Grandfather was a farmer. Father is a farmer. I'll be a farmer. The end.' Bet your mom and dad can beat that. Anyone can."

As soon as he said it he realized his mistake. Everyone knew Lizzie's mom had died right after Lizzie was born. That's why hardly anyone at school talked to her. They didn't know what to say. At least, that's why they'd started off not talking to her. Then she'd become withdrawn and silent and nobody wanted to make the effort to play with her. They decided she was 'stuck up' and left her alone. Friends and alliances had been made and it was suddenly too late for Lizzie to become a part of anything or anyone.

"I mean, um…", he trailed off.

"It's okay. Actually, I think I've found some cool stuff. I don't know yet. It's just a lot of stuff in boxes right now. I need to organize it a bit."

"Neat!" Bobby was relieved. "Let me know if you need help!" He had no idea why he'd said that. Just something to keep the conversation moving, anything to get it away from him mentioning her dead mom.

"Sure," replied Lizzie, while privately planning to never let him anywhere near the boxes. This was her story, not his. "So I'd best be going. Thanks for showing me the canoe. It's great."

Bobby saw a long, empty summer stretching

ahead of him and leapt in. "Come back tomorrow? After lunch? We'll go again."

"Okay." She smiled at him, waved an awkward goodbye, and walked back to her bike.

Mrs. Dabble was secretly delighted that Lizzie seemed to have made a friend.

"The Bingles are wonderful folk," she enthused. "Been here for generations. I helped Mrs. B before the three boys were old enough for school. Makes a lovely jam, she does."

Lizzie told her about learning to canoe and showed Mrs. Dabble her blistered hands.

"You know what you want to do for that?" asked Mrs. Dabble.

Lizzie pressed the blisters and shook her head.

"Well, it sounds odd but many people swear by it. When you go to the bathroom you want to... Well, you want to pee on your hands."

Lizzie's jaw hit the floor. For one, Mrs. Dabble had used the word 'pee', and she'd never said that before. For two, this was disgusting.

Mrs. Dabble held her hands up defensively. "I

know, I know! Sounds horrible but it works to toughen up your hands. Or you can just use a bit of this," and she handed Lizzie a jar of vaseline and some bandages.

With hands suitably bound, Lizzie climbed back into the attic, laid out her pens and highlighters, and hauled the first of the 'mercury' boxes across to the window. At least that opened more easily the second time round.

After an hour she had sorted the papers into a few piles: newspaper articles, court documents, photographs, and 'other' (which was a ragtag assortment of letters, posters and handwritten, almost illegible notes on thin, yellowing paper). It didn't feel as if she were any further forwards, to be honest, and she still didn't have a clue what to do. And there was no space in the attic. There was stuff everywhere and she kept banging her head on the sloping ceiling. Even with her magnifying glass hovering over the documents, she still couldn't read some of them in the low light.

Lizzie picked at her bandages and decided she'd just have to ask Dad for help.

She waited by the front door until he came home from work, sitting on the steps and idling the time by piling up stones into little towers.

He was back late, arriving only as the sun made the sky into streaks of orange and red, transforming the distant trees into silhouettes where the chattering sparrows finally turned in for the night and the owls started to hoot.

"Hey, Busy Lizzie," he smiled. Tired. He put his briefcase on the step beside her and sat down. "Nice towers," he said, pointing towards the stones.

"How do you organize your work, Dad?" she asked. "I mean, when you get a new case, how do you start figuring out what happened?"

"I start at the beginning."

Why hadn't she thought of that?

"How do you know where the beginning is?" she asked him.

He looked down at his daughter. That, he decided, was a very sensible question. Not such an easy one to answer. How far back should you go in a case? He thought about Irene Ward. About her childhood. Can you be blamed for being the person your parents created? Where does the buck stop? He had spent so long trying to protect Lizzie from the realities of the world, hiding her away in a small town far from everything, and here she was, asking questions that showed she knew there was something else –

something more.

"The beginning is the moment before it all goes wrong," he finally concluded.

Lizzie tucked that thought away in her mind, and realized she didn't even know what had gone wrong yet. She knew it was something to do with mercury and fish but that was about it. Maybe she would ask Bobby to help after all.

CHAPTER 4

BY THE LIGHT OF THE MOON

“**O**h, definitely!”

Bobby was happy Lizzie had come back. He was happy she'd gone in the canoe again, even with her hands covered in bandages. And he was happy she'd asked him to help with the project. Anything, anything, to fill the long days – even if it sounded a bit too much like schoolwork.

“We can use the old barn. Nobody goes in there, loads of space.”

Lizzie looked doubtful. “It's dry? I don't want anything damaged.”

“Come and see for yourself!” He pulled her up from the grass, held her hand a moment longer than was needed, turned bright red and dropped it like a hot potato. “Follow me!” he shouted and ran off fast to cover his embarrassment.

Lizzie raced after him, long legs and arms flailing as they ran down the hillside. Her too-big dress flapped around her like a sail. Why did Dad always buy such awful clothes? Lizzie never wanted to hurt his feelings – and really, she didn't care so very much what she wore – but sometimes she wished he could give her something that actually fitted. And that wasn't grey or military green.

Bobby hauled open the huge barn doors and she peered inside. A vast, empty space looked back at her, more than enough room to spread out all the papers in a bid to find 'the moment before it all went wrong' and the beginning of the story.

It was perfect.

"The thing is," she admitted to Bobby, "I don't really want Dad to know what I'm doing. He's got a big case on right now and this is all stuff to do with my Mom. I don't want to make him sad. Can you come over and help me sneak everything out, do you think?"

"I'm your man," grinned Bobby. "Totally up for sneaky stuff. Tonight any good?"

She nodded.

"Great. It's a date."

He instantly went bright red again. What was it with this girl?

Back at home, Lizzie lay in bed, adrenaline keeping her awake. As the clock struck midnight, she crept downstairs and let Bobby into the house.

"Your parents didn't hear you leave?" she whispered to him.

Bobby shook his head.

Something had been troubling her. "Why are we doing this at night?"

"It's just what always happens in movies," he whispered back.

Lizzie rolled her eyes. Maybe asking for Bobby's help wasn't such a great idea after all, if all he wanted to do was create unnecessary drama.

They tiptoed up the stairs, Lizzie pointing to the step that creaked loudly and motioning for him to avoid it. Up in the attic she showed him the big boxes. Then pointed out the chalkboard she'd found in the shadows, the one she'd had as a little girl and now stowed away with her old rocking horse and clothes that had (finally) become too small for her to wear. "We must give these away," her father said to her, sighing, every time he added another carefully folded pile. Lizzie always privately thought the clothes were perhaps best left abandoned in the attic.

"You want that as well?"

"Shhh!" She put a finger to her lips.

"You want that as well?" he repeated in a whisper.

Lizzie nodded. And pointed towards the backpack, filled with all the things she'd bought and would need in order to be a proper detective.

"We'll need two trips, then," he whispered.

Lizzie shrugged. She didn't need someone putting obstacles in her path.

Bobby pulled out the top photograph from a box and shone his flashlight on it. The determined look in the woman's eyes that stared back at him was one he'd seen on Lizzie's face.

"Your grandmother?"

"Great-grandmother. Marion."

She cast her eyes back to the boxes and looked back at him. Yup, there it was. That look that said, "We've something to do here, let's just get on with it."

Bobby looked at the man in the picture. In another one, it showed the man standing beside a huge haul of fish, cigar sticking out from his smile. "Barney," it said on the back of the photo.

As they crept down the stairs, each with a box in their arms, Bobby forgot about the creaky step. They both stopped, horrified by how loud the sound was in the silent, sleeping house. Leaning back against the wall they hardly dared to breathe. Waiting for a door to open, a light to go on, a 'who goes there?' to be called.

Nothing came but a loud rumble from Bobby's stomach.

Lizzie glared at Bobby in the dark. "You're hungry *now*?" she hissed.

"Sorry...".

Minutes passed, her dad didn't appear, and they continued down the stairs. Their feet scrunched on the gravel outside, every sound exaggerated by the silence of the night. They walked without speaking, Lizzie struggling with the heavy box but refusing to stop as long as Bobby kept going. He saw her shifting the weight around and took pity on her.

"Let's just look at the moon for a minute," he said, putting his box on the ground and folding his arms to show he was staying there for a while.

Lizzie suspected he didn't really care about looking at the moon at all but gratefully lowered her box, too.

There was a complete stillness to the world. No wind rustled the trees, even the owls seemed to have given up their hunting. The road stretched ahead, a single silver stroke in the darkness. In the distance, Lizzie could see the moon reflected in the lake by Bobby's house. Something – a frog, probably – moved in the water and for a few moments the reflection was a mass of ripples, a hall-of-mirrors mockery of the moon that eventually settled back into a calm, perfect disc. There was something magic, feeling as if you were the only two people left in the world, the only two who knew about this moment, this place. Lizzie imagined what it must be like to see the night in a big city: all neon lights and belching buses rattling around their routes, thumping music climbing out from behind closed doors, streetlights hiding the silver moon. Out here, in the perfect stillness, you could find peace.

Bobby spent the time looking at Lizzie. In school she always seemed so tense and nervous, hunched up against the world. But outside, the worry left her face, she stood a little taller, she seemed more sure of herself.

"Come on," he eventually said. "Let's get this thing done."

When they went back to get the chalkboard Bobby said he'd carry it himself. He balanced it on top of his head, arms up to hold it in place, and mouthed 'goodnight' as he turned and headed off across the gravel for a second time.

Lizzie caught up with him as he reached the end of the driveway and slipped a large piece of Mrs. Dabble's cake into his pocket.

"For the journey," she said and smiled before rushing back indoors to hide from her own boldness.

CHAPTER 5

MEETING A WHIRLWIND

Bobby threw open the barn doors and got just the reaction he wanted.

"Um, wow. I mean, WOW." Lizzie smiled at him. "Thank you!"

He'd spent the whole morning heaving hay bales around to form tables and chairs for them. The blackboard was in place with the chalk lined up neatly, ready for use. The roll of sticky tape hung on a nearby nail. And he'd tacked a huge map of Canada on the wall (stolen from his brother's bedroom). A large red pin marked a spot.

"What's that?" Lizzie asked.

"That," he said proudly, "is where Ball Lake Lodge is. Was. Is. Whatever it is, that's the lodge."

Lizzie ran her fingers across the map and read out the names. Grassy Narrows. Whitedog. Silver Lake.

Wonderland Lake. Eagle Dogtooth.

"Doesn't it sound magical?" she said to him.

"I also borrowed these from my brother. I mean, he's away so he won't care," Bobby said. "Thought they might, you know, be useful."

He pointed towards a small pile of books on the table and she looked quickly at the titles. Anything and everything to do with the First Nations, including a rather alarming looking one on hunting techniques. Lizzie picked up the one with a brightly painted eagle on its cover.

"The Ojibwe," she read out slowly, rolling the awkward name around her mouth. "Ha, it says their name means 'The Puckered Moccasin People'. I like that."

"It could also mean 'those who keep records'," Bobby said. In response to her surprised look he said, "Yeah, I sort of couldn't sleep last night so did a bit of reading. About the Ojibwe," he hastily added, before she thought he'd been going through the boxes.

"What else do you know about them?" she asked curiously.

"Well, they've lived here for hundreds of years. They first met Europeans in 1615, it's reckoned. A

French explorer called Samuel something-or-other. Basically, once the Europeans arrived in Canada and America, it was harder and harder for the Ojibwe to carry on how they'd always lived. They live off the land, you see. Hunting and fishing. Trapping. They eat a lot of wild rice – and berries, they know all about which berries to eat.

"Some time in the 1800s – I'm really bad at dates, I can't remember stuff like that – they signed an agreement with the English that said they could always use the land for hunting and fishing. So they could keep living how they wanted. But since, like, the 1950s, people have realized that these guys are living on some valuable land. Logging companies want it. A lot. So the Ojibwe have been fighting, saying that it isn't fair. They say they were told they could always live their traditional way of life.

"Apparently, the people at Grassy Narrows had to lie down in the road for years to stop logging companies coming onto their land. Crazy, right? They didn't even want to live where they do now. The government made them move.

"Oh, and mercury really messed them up. It got into the fish, and because they eat a lot of fish it made them sick."

Lizzie pricked up her ears.

"You read stuff about mercury?"

"Well, just that really. That there's a lot of mercury in the rivers and lakes around where they live and it's really bad for you. So, you know, don't eat mercury-laced fish. Seems simple."

"But if they don't eat fish, what else do they eat?"

"Berries? And they can hunt. They can hunt for moose and stuff?"

"I guess," Lizzie said. "But –" she was the stubborn sort and was going to get to the bottom of this, "You can't just eat berries, can you? I mean, for one, they don't grow all year. And for two, you have to eat an awful lot of berries to make up for not eating fish."

"Fine, eat a moose then."

"Right. But. What if you run out of moose? If you're suddenly eating all the moose, there won't be any left will there?"

Bobby looked at her. This girl could argue.

"I don't know," he shrugged. "But now I'm hungry."

"Good timing, then!" smiled Mrs. Bingle as she walked into the barn carrying a tray piled high with sandwiches, cookies and a huge jug of lemonade. She set it down on the hay bale. "Hello, dear," she said to

46

Lizzie. "Lovely to meet you. I've seen you around, of course, but we've never properly spoken have we? I'm Bobby's mom. You can call me Sheila."

"Hi, Mrs. B – I mean, Sheila," Lizzie said awkwardly and stretched out her hand.

"Oh come here, dear." Mrs. Bingle grabbed Lizzie and drew her in for a hug. She smelled of the kitchen, all cinnamon and apples and freshly baked bread, and when she finally released Lizzie she'd transferred flour from her floral apron all over Lizzie's grey dress.

"Just look at you! I'm so sorry," Mrs. Bingle cheerfully patted away at the ballooning dress, sending up little clouds of white flour dust. She was rosy cheeked with the brightest, bluest eyes Lizzie had ever seen, hair tied back in two braids that were somehow wrapped together to form a crown.

"I love your hair, Mrs. Bingle," stammered Lizzie. She wasn't used to people, and especially wasn't used to strangers who reached out and hugged her. "It looks awfully nice done like that."

"Thank you, dear. It's Sheila. Let me just…" and Mrs. Bingle spun Lizzie round, her hands flew back and forth, and suddenly Lizzie's hair was just the same – a little burnished gold crown. Everything happened so fast Lizzie didn't have a chance to back away.

"That'll help keep the hair out of your eyes as you work," said Mrs. Bingle. "And let me just..." – she reached over and rolled up the bulky sleeves of the dress, rustled around in her apron pocket for a moment and pulled out a length of ribbon that she quickly slipped around Lizzie's waist before spinning her and tying it into a bow.

"There! Now you don't need to worry about that getting in the way, either," she smiled kindly. "Mrs. Dabble doing well, is she? Yes? Lovely." She reached over and tweaked the dress a little, aligning the newly created pleats. "Do say hello to Mrs. Dabble from me, won't you?"

Lizzie barely had time to nod.

"Bobby? Make sure you don't eat ALL the sandwiches," Mrs. Bingle said over her shoulder as she was leaving.

"Wow. She's amazing," said Lizzie. "She's like a whirlwind. Only in a good way. Puts things together instead of tearing them apart."

"That's Mom," replied Bobby through a mouthful of bread and cheese. He swallowed. "Right, where do we begin?" He pointed towards the boxes.

"At the beginning. Dad said you always start at the beginning. I sorted it all out into different types of information before – see, there's a pile of newspapers, and this one has a pile of letters in it – but I think that's wrong. We need to organize it all by dates. So let's use this end" – she pointed to the far end of the long, hay-bale table – "for the earliest stuff, and come up to here" – she ran to the other end of the hay bales – "for the most recent stuff. Got it?"

"Got it."

And so they set to work, Lizzie trying to focus while pushing back the memory of how it felt when Mrs. Bingle had hugged her, and the easy way Bobby and his mother had worked silently, familiarly, together to transfer everything from tray to hay-bale table.

For once, Lizzie was pleased when Mrs. Dabble announced that Dad wanted to have dinner with her. She decided she would start the conversation this time. With all the reading she'd been doing, something was playing on her mind.

Mrs. Dabble was a little taken aback by this new

version of Lizzie that came into her kitchen. She seemed taller, all of a sudden. She held her head high. Look at those braids! Look at the ribbon on her dress! Mrs. Dabble guessed that Bobby Bingle's mother had been involved: it was the sort of thing she'd do but Mrs. Dabble had never dared.

"You're looking very well, Lizzie," was the best she could muster. "That canoeing must be good for you."

"Canoeing? Oh, yes. Canoeing."

There hadn't been any time for canoeing, not after they'd sorted every single piece of paper in the boxes. Bobby had needed to fetch another two hay bales to extend the table. The earliest thing they'd found was the photograph of Barney and Marion Lamm on their wedding day, back in 1946. There were references in newspapers to Barney's earlier life, growing up on a farm called Green Gables, but the oldest single item was that photo.

The documents stopped in the late 2000s. That would have been when Lizzie's mother died and there was nobody left to put anything more into the boxes. One of the last pieces came from 2002, an obituary of Barney Lamm in a Winnipeg newspaper. Lizzie read about her great-grandfather's humour and generosity and kindness, about how he loved flying, about how he and his wife had run the greatest, most luxurious fishing lodge in Canada.

She wished she could have met him, this man with the smile and the cigar. She wished she could have known her great-grandmother, too. She looked at the photographs of this couple and the wonderful, adventurous life they had lived together, and she thought about her father and how he had lost his chance of just such a wonderful life when her mother had died. Lizzie hardly ever felt sorry for herself – when you've grown up without a mother you don't really know any different – but for a moment she wondered what it would have been like to live with the energy of a lady who had descended from Marion. She reached up and felt the braids wound around her head. "That's what it would feel like," she thought to herself, remembering the whirlwind of activity that accompanied Mrs. Bingle.

And so it was time for dinner, and Lizzie walked in and loved seeing the surprise on her father's face when he noted the braids.

"Your hair looks lovely, Busy Lizzie," he said to her. "Where did you learn to do that?"

"It was Bobby's mom," she replied, and then

rushed in with her question before he could start asking her what she was doing hanging around with Bobby Bingle. "Dad, do you think I have mercury poisoning?"

He set down his fork and looked at her curiously.

"Do I think you have mercury poisoning?" he repeated.

"Yes. You see, I was reading about the symptoms and I think I have some. I mean, sometimes I'm sad. And sometimes, I can't remember things. And once, I dropped a cup for no reason at all, so I wondered…". She trailed off.

Dad burst out laughing.

"My dearest, darlingest Lizzie," he eventually said. "I can categorically state, with no question of being wrong, that you do not have mercury poisoning. Whatever gave you that idea?"

While relieved and a little annoyed at the same time – it's never fun to be laughed at – Lizzie decided not to tell the whole truth.

"It's just a school project I'm doing," she said. "Mercury. We're learning about mercury. Not the planet. The metal, the stuff they put in thermometers. Quicksilver."

"This isn't anything to do with the family history,

is it?"

Without looking up from her plate she sensed his single raised eyebrow.

"Well, not exactly." (It was a half-lie. That was fine, right? If it was to stop him thinking about things that would make him unhappy?). "Just mercury, really. It's metal but it's a silver liquid unless you get it really, really cold. Kind of amazing."

She was going off on a tangent to lead him away from thoughts of the family, and it seemed to work.

"Talk to someone with mercury poisoning, they'll tell you how it really is," he said to her. And with that, he settled back to spearing his potatoes and hunting cherry tomatoes on the plate and trying to distract himself from the little girl at the end of the table who was becoming more like her mother with every passing day. He suspected she was lying and, privately, he thanked her for it. It was a coward's way of being her parent, he knew that, but some things he didn't want to face. Not today, not ever.

The likes of Irene Ward kept him distracted. Safe. Safe from his past. A horrifying present was infinitely better than a heartbreaking past.

As Lizzie climbed into bed that night, a plan was beginning to form.

CHAPTER 6

A PLAN TAKES SHAPE

B obby was already waiting for her in the barn when she arrived the next morning. Lizzie dropped her bike carelessly in the doorway – the bell gave a little 'ding!' of pain as it hit the ground – and raced in.

"Bobby! I've got it!"

She tugged in a mouthful of air.

"We've got to go there!"

Sucking up another great lungful of air.

"The lodge!"

She pointed to the map and dramatically collapsed on a hay bale.

Bobby stood up and gestured towards the neat row of papers they had organized only the day before.

"And what about all this?" he asked, sweeping his hand the length of the table. "Don't you think we've got enough here?"

"Oh, we need to read all that, too," she assured him. "But we've also got to go there. Dad always says that you have to meet people who are involved in a case. It's the only way of really getting to know them. So, we've got to meet people."

"They're dead," said Bobby, flatly.

"Not Barney and Marion. The people at Grassy Narrows. The ones still living there. Maybe even people who worked at the lodge. Don't you see? Look at these reports. They show people are still getting sick from the mercury. They're still living with it. We've got to talk to them."

Bobby felt a little jump of excitement. A proper adventure! His brothers would be green when they came back and found out how he'd spent his summer. Milking cows? Ha! Not a bit of it.

"But you're right, Bobby. We need to read through all of this."

He could have kicked himself. He'd fallen right into that one. It would take days to read through everything here, never mind understand it. His heart was already in a canoe somewhere in Canada.

"I'm going to work forwards," Lizzie announced, heading down to the far end of the barn. "And you work backwards."

"Backwards?"

"Yes, backwards. I think it's a good idea. Maybe we'll miss something if we both do it the same way. Working backwards is fine. Lawyers like Dad do it all the time," she added airily, not entirely sure if it was true but it sounded like it should be.

They agreed to work until lunchtime and then compare notes, each taking up a pile of colorful sticky tabs as they went to their separate ends of the makeshift table. Working in silence, they steadily read each page. Bobby got up and left at one point and came back bearing an enormous dictionary. Occasionally one of them would let out a quiet, 'huh!' After a while, Lizzie started writing on the chalk-board. In the center, circled a few times for emphasis, she put 'Dryden'. Bobby gave her a thumbs up when he saw that then got back to his reading.

Mrs. Bingle interrupted them just after midday, this time carrying a tray with huge chunks of pie and a veritable forest of salad leaves.

"How's it all going?" she asked.

"Hi, Mrs. B. We're getting somewhere, I think. Have you ever heard of Dryden mill?"

Mrs. Bingle shook her head.

"It's up in Canada, in northwestern Ontario. In the 1960s, they started dumping mercury into the English-Wabigoon River. The mercury was used to bleach pulp that was later made into paper, you see, and they just dumped it into the river."

Mrs. Bingle's eyes opened wide.

"But isn't that rather dangerous, dear?"

"Very!" said Bobby. "It's crazy, Mom. You should read about Minamata in Japan."

"I've heard of that..." she said, vaguely, unconvincingly.

"Mercury poisoning is called Minamata disease because of what happened there. Basically, this factory was dumping mercury into Minamata Bay, and people got really sick from eating all the fish they caught there. Like, really, really sick. They figured it out in the 1950s, that it was mercury in the fish that made people ill."

"Wait," interrupted Lizzie. "They knew about this in the 1950s? But Dryden was dumping stuff in the 60s. And they didn't know it was dangerous?"

Bobby shrugged. "I'm going backwards, remember. I just got sidetracked and read some stuff about Minamata because it's in Japan." He did a quick karate chop in the air. "Cool stuff comes from Japan," he confirmed.

"Are you sure the dates are right, dear?" Mrs. Bingle asked Lizzie. Lizzie checked back through the pages, running her finger quickly down the para- graphs.

"Hundred percent. Listen. "It was in 1962 that the Dryden Chemical Company... began to discharge mercury waste into the English-Wabigoon River system." That's in a paper sent to the government in Ontario by the former Grand Chief."

"Remind me where you got all this stuff, Lizzie?"

"It was my mother's. It's been up in the attic for years. My great-grandparents had a lodge on a lake and they had to close down because of all the mercury there. The fish weren't safe to eat. They used to do these shore lunches, you see. People went up to catch fish and the guides would cook the fish and eat with them. Then they'd take more fish home, too. So while a visitor would eat fish for a week or so and not get that much mercury, the guides were eating it for months. They had crazy amounts of mercury."

"It's more than that," said Bobby. "Much more. Marion, that's her great-grandmother, did a load of research and it's ended up at Harvard, in the library. It's called – wait, let me find it – the Marion Lamm

Mercury Collection. They got fifty-nine boxes of stuff she gathered up about mercury and mercury poisoning. That must have taken her years." He looked across at the few boxes they had and heaved a sigh of relief that fifty-nine of the things hadn't been stored in the attic. They'd never have been able to read it all.

"So Marion found out about it all? Why her?" Lizzie was impressed.

"It looks like Barney – Lizzie's great-grandfather – was trying to get money from the government. Not just for him, but for the people of Grassy Narrows. He tried to get money out of the Dryden Pulp and Paper Mill people, too. It looks like he was mad he had to close down. He lost money. The guides lost money. The guides were sick, and Barney was paying for research into the mercury and how bad the poisoning was. Maybe Marion was helping him fight the government?"

Mrs. Bingle quietly slipped out and left them to it. Whatever was going on in there, it made her head hurt more than a little and, beyond providing cake and lemonade every now and then, she was pretty sure she couldn't be of much use. She touched her stomach and felt a hard kick from within. Mrs. Bingle loved her three boys, but every time the child inside moved she secretly prayed for a little girl this time.

Lizzie grabbed a stick and walked over to her chalkboard.

"It's all starting to make sense now," she said, enthusiastically punctuating each of her points by jabbing at the board with the stick. "Dryden mill" – thwack! – "started pouring mercury into the river, even though they should have known better. Barney and Marion" – thwack! – "decided to close the lodge because it wasn't safe to eat the fish. The government" – thwack! – "said it would be safe within twelve weeks but Barney didn't believe them. So he and Marion" – thwack! – "got some scientists in to check it out."

Bobby grabbed the stick off her, gulped down his mouthful of pie, and took her place.

"And the government said they didn't know it was dangerous but that's not true because it had already happened in Minamata" – thwack! – "and they must have known. And anyway, they had rules about how much mercury could be in fish, so they must have known it was dangerous." He stopped and drew a crazy-looking fish on the board, and gave that a firm 'thwack!' too for good measure. "In 2021, the government gave money to start building a clinic to help people from Grassy Narrows and Whitedog who were sick. They've given $90 million now for this care home. Sort of shows they're feeling guilty, I'd say."

He threw the stick at her feet.

"Oh," he added, "I read somewhere that there was a deal done. The people at Grassy got the lodge, and Barney got a million dollars. They tried to run the lodge for a few years but I guess it's kind of hard to run a fishing lodge when nobody can eat the fish, and when you don't have any experience of running a place like that...".

They both sat back on their hay bales, a little exhausted.

It was Lizzie who broke the silence.

"I think I want to know more about the lodge. I want to know more about Barney and Marion. And I want to know what has been done to help everyone living in Grassy Narrows and Whitedog."

Bobby nodded. "Looks like you had some pretty amazing great-grandparents, Lizzie. I doubt mine had even heard of Harvard, and there's Marion with a special collection in their library. And look at this lot" – he pointed to a stack of papers – "they're all obituaries written about Barney. You should read them, you know."

"It's all a bit much," said Lizzie. "Can we go in the canoe for a bit?"

They walked down to the lake and Lizzie climbed in, less worried now by the rocking motion. This time, it was almost soothing, like being rocked gently to sleep. She lay back and looked at the sky and let Bobby do the paddling. Normally, he liked to race around the lake as fast as he could but today he took it slowly, dipping the paddle into the water as quietly as possible and taking care not to flick any drops of water her way when he switched sides. Lizzie's mind eventually slowed as she stared at the clear blue sky and listened to the water bubble gently beneath the canoe.

Lizzie may have calmed down but Bobby's mind was still working. He'd been looking at the map and getting to Ball Lake would be no easy mission. There was a reason Barney used to fly everything and everyone in there: it was impossible to reach by any other way. He pushed the blade into the water and wondered just how far he could paddle…

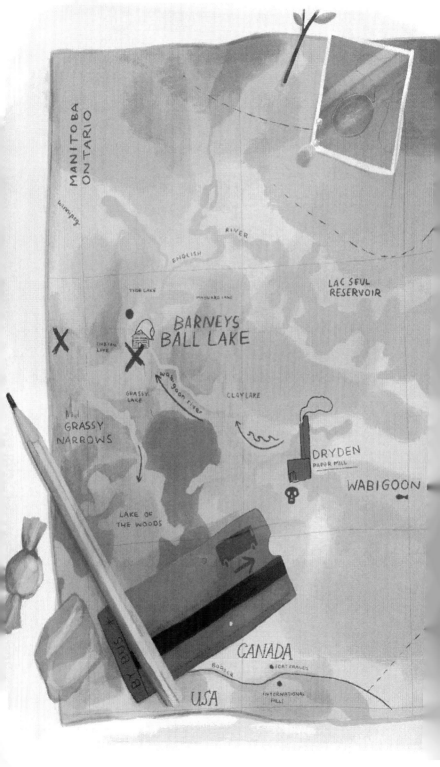

CHAPTER 7

LITTLE LIES

Mrs. Dabble was sitting outside in a deckchair when Lizzie came home that evening.

Lizzie nodded, leaned her bike against the wall and lay down on the grass next to the old lady's chair.

"Isn't watching the sky just wonderful?" she said to Mrs. Dabble.

Mrs. Dabble wasn't quite sure it was really that wonderful but she was prepared to agree it wasn't a terrible way to spend a few minutes. Mrs. Dabble preferred, all in all, to be doing things. "Making progress," she called it. She found immense satisfaction in polishing the dining table until it glinted in the sunlight, or making the beds with crisp perfection, clamping the corners in hard so that every night when Lizzie got in she had to thrash around for a while to loosen the sheets. Mrs. Dabble knew how to arrange flowers and bake a cake and get tomato sauce off the carpet but there her skills ended. She'd never really known what to do with Lizzie and the girl seemed to be getting wilder by the day. Today she even had a garland of daises around her head. Whatever next?

"Do you have a bus timetable, Mrs. Dabble?"

She started.

"A bus timetable? Whatever do you want that for?"

"Oh it isn't for me, it's for Bobby." A small white lie.

"That boy. He'll be the death of his mother, the mischief he gets into sometimes. There's a timetable in my bag if you fetch it for me."

Lizzie smiled. Mrs. Dabble's handbag contained at least one of everything, it sometimes seemed.

Running her finger down the sheet Lizzie found what she was after: buses into Milwaukee. They'd have to change in Elkhorn but that was fine, she'd been there with Dad a few times and it wasn't a very big place at all.

"He's asked me to go camping. Isn't that fun?" It sounded awkwardly false to her but Mrs. Dabble wasn't paying much attention. That knitting pattern back at home was proving to be an absolute devil and her mind was busy click-clacking away with the needles, trying to work out where she'd been going wrong.

"Sounds fun. Mention it to your father," she replied, and felt that her job was done.

Years before, Lizzie's broken father had sought Mrs. Dabble out, asking for her help in caring for the little girl. And she had looked at the bundle he held in his arms, seen the desperation in his eyes, and taken the job. There were days when she had been utterly frustrated by the pair, with Lizzie's father coming back later and later from work and leaving her to drive home in the dark. Times when she wondered how Lizzie could bear the silence that seemed to surround her – a silence that Mrs. Dabble only knew how to break with the clattering of cutlery or exaggerated huffing and puffing as she cleaned.

Had she always thought of Lizzie as something apart, something special? Not really, but that wasn't going to stop her telling all her friends. "I've always said," she could be heard announcing over a pot of tea at Lillian's Cafe in the weeks and months that followed the events of that summer, "that the girl was special. Always said it. Always knew. Didn't I always say it? She just had an air about her, you know?" And the friends would nod enthusiastically and keep her little lies safe and say kindly, "Oh, you did, you always did."

For the world turns on such little lies. It spins around to the things left unsaid, the spaces and the silence.

Lizzie did try to speak to her father a few days later. She'd started by asking him about the locket she wore, and what photo her mother would have had inside when she'd worn it.

"I don't remember," he'd said a touch too quickly.

"Really? But you said before that she always wore it, and that –"

"No. I just don't remember." He cut her off and she decided that was that. If he wasn't going to tell her about her mother and her family, she'd have to find out for herself.

So while Lizzie was busy working out how to get to Milwaukee, Bobby went back into his brother's room and took down the map of the US, too. Out in the barn he picked up the red string and marked their route: Elkhorn, Milwaukee, Minneapolis, International Falls, Kenora, Ball Lake Lodge. Lizzie had insisted on paying for everything – "It's my family, and you're helping me, and what else am I supposed to spend years of saved up pocket money on?" – but he was still careful to search for the cheapest way to get between places. When you grow up without money, spending is never easy – whoever's paying.

He wasn't looking forward to telling Lizzie it would be almost impossible to get to Whitedog. Grassy Narrows was going to be tough enough, and he hoped that would satisfy her.

"We're going camping," he'd announced to his parents. "Lizzie's never been and she really wants to try it, so I said I'd take her."

"On the farm, dear? That'll be nice."

"No, I thought we'd do it properly. You know, take a tent, carry our stuff. Take the stove. She likes being outside."

His mother frowned and felt a little niggle of worry.

"Good lad!" said Bobby's father, slapping him on the back. "Bit of camping? Best thing in the world. And if this Lizzie of yours doesn't have a sleeping bag," he added gallantly, "she can borrow mine."

Mrs. Bingle gave in. "I'll bake a cake," she sighed. She'd never understand why people got so terribly excited about sleeping in an uncomfortable bed with no bathroom nearby. There was enough nature right here on the farm for her liking. It was with an uneasy feeling she stirred the batter. She liked Lizzie – the girl had a steady determination about her that was rare these days – but all this talk of mercury and lawsuits and 'getting even' that she'd heard recently was a little alarming.

The child inside Mrs. Bingle gave a couple of kicks, and the worry was soon forgotten as thoughts of sun dresses and flowery hats crowded it out.

CHAPTER 8

FINDING FIREFLY

It turns out that it's a long way to Kenora.

In fact, it's a long way to Minneapolis, too. Nearly eight hours on a bus, to be exact. Fortunately, they were catching the night bus.

"That means that a, we don't need to work out where to stay overnight," announced Bobby, "and b, it'll be dark when we get on so maybe the driver won't see that we aren't, you know, grown ups."

Lizzie hadn't even thought of that, but Bobby was right. Nobody paid them much attention, not least because she was wearing a large, grey dress that was about as anonymous an outfit as anybody could sport.

Bobby had been the one to organize the trip. He'd piled up the tent and stove and water bottles and a whole load of things Lizzie couldn't identify. Handing her his brother's backpack, he told her to stick some clothes in it, wear some sensible shoes, and showed her how to strap a roll-mat to the outside with elastic cords. She'd done as he'd told her and then, hidden away in some extra socks, she'd carefully stowed a cigar she slipped from the box in her father's study. That would be her secret for later.

The bus pulled into Minneapolis in the grey light of dawn. Lizzie had been able to sleep by curling herself tight into a ball in her seat, her head resting on Bobby's shoulder. That head meant Bobby had barely been able to sleep at all.

"We'll get there, won't we?" she'd asked him, half asleep, as she'd settled herself down.

"We'll get there. I promise. And a promise is a promise," he'd told her.

She'd given a small smile, mumbled a 'thank you', and slept soundly in the safety of his promise.

Emerging from the bustle of the bus station, Lizzie looked up at the gleaming skyscrapers – they really did reach towards the sky – and felt tiny. Everywhere there was noise, cars rushed by far faster than she'd ever seen back at home. A florist carried out buckets of bright blooms and people in suits grabbed papers from the newsstand as they rushed past. Everyone seemed to have somewhere to be and they were in a terrible hurry to get there, their stretched early-morning shadows jostling for position on the sidewalk. Lizzie thought about 'town' and the four storefronts, where people idled and chatted and shared apples in the autumn and radishes in the spring. No wonder Dad looked so tired the days he had to go to his offices in Chicago.

Bobby came back from the counter brandishing another pair of tickets.

"Five hours to International Falls," he grinned. "Bus goes in an hour. Breakfast?" He held out two giant muffins, one bursting with purple blueberries and the other spattered with chocolate drops. "I didn't know which you'd like best. Blueberries? Good choice."

Lizzie had gone back to being quiet, he noticed. Was it the city? Was it him? Had she decided the trip was a bad idea? Bobby decided it was probably best not to know – there was no way he was backing out of this adventure now – and he'd just do the talking for her instead. He didn't want to alarm her but there was the small matter of getting from the States into Canada, and although he had a plan he wasn't quite sure she'd be happy to go along with it. Best just keep her moving, keep distracting her, and pretend everything was fine.

They were lucky with the next bus driver, too. The lady raised an eyebrow when they boarded but Bobby pointed vaguely to the back of the bus and told her that their parents were already sitting down. If you say something in a convincing way, turns out people will often believe you.

It worked on Lizzie, too, once they finally arrived at International Falls.

"People borrow other people's canoes all the time," he said in as casual and off-hand a manner as he could muster. "It's the done thing. Seriously. People are always walking onto the farm and heading to our lake and just going out in ours."

"It sounds like stealing," she said.

"Honestly, it's just... borrowing. For a bit. When we come back, we'll put the canoe right where we find it. I'll bet they won't even notice it's gone. Besides, do you have a better idea for how to get into Canada?"

Lizzie did not, and it was something she instantly regretted. In all the chaos and excitement and feeling of being a Great Adventurer, she'd forgotten about practicalities. She'd read how Barney and Marion had simply climbed into their little two-seater back in

1946 and flown up to Ball Lake to start cutting down trees and build their lodge. Times had changed. Now there were rules about these things; you couldn't just go where you wanted on a whim. She imagined the two of them, newly married, climbing into the plane, Barney up front and Marion right behind, ready for a water landing and a new life. They must have been terribly brave.

In which case she, Lizzie, could be brave too. She'd had twelve years of being not-very-brave and the last week had been the most exciting of her life.

"Look on it as a story to tell our great-grandchildren," Bobby said, instantly regretting the use of 'our' and once more turning into a beetroot. "I mean, yours and mine. I mean, you know, the ones you have and the ones I'll have separately. Different ones. Different entirely. Ha! Imagine."

He needn't have worried; she was tuned out to him anyway. Lizzie had made up her mind. She swung left and right, made an instant decision purely based on liking the color of a house she saw to her left, and marched off. "Come on, then!" she called over her shoulder.

Bobby trotted alongside her, demanding only a small detour to purchase food supplies before starting to seriously eye up the little docks. All manner of boats were tied up but he wanted a canoe, something he knew how to steer and maneuver.

"There!" Lizzie pointed. "And she's called 'Firefly'. Isn't that beautiful? She'll take us across, I'm sure of it."

He was already doubting his own plan but Lizzie had clearly bought the idea: her backpack was sitting in the center of the canoe and she was busy fiddling with the knot that tied it to the dock.

"Oh, let me. You get in," he told her, looking anxiously at water that was an awful lot more choppy than any on the lake had ever been. His nervous hands fumbled with the knot and by the time he pushed off from the small dock he was shaking.

"Lizzie? You're up. Let's paddle!"

CHAPTER 9

THE FLOWERS AND THE FROG

It was hard to know which of the two was more surprised when they set foot on the other side. Both of them hid it well. Lizzie just casually said, "Oh, looks like we're here," and Bobby said, "Yup, easy as pie" as he wobbled his way onto a grassy bank and pulled the canoe close.

"Told you we'd be fine," he added, reassurance to himself as much as to her. "Next stop: Kenora."

"Couldn't we, you know, just stay here for the night?"

He looked at Lizzie and saw she was exhausted. They'd both been running on adrenaline and were a little overwhelmed by what they'd done. Lizzie was in a new country for the first time ever. She'd seen a big city. They'd ridden buses for hours and hours. And both of them were sort of criminals for taking that boat. Lizzie could imagine Dad's voice. "Sort of criminals? You either are or you aren't – and in this case, you very much are I'm afraid." Surely, she thought, there are different types of right and wrong. The law wasn't – Dad's voice interrupted again. "It is. The law is black and white."

Bobby pointed to a group of trees. "We'll camp in there," he said. "Nice and quiet. Nobody will spot us."

She watched as he put up the tent, held the pegs as he banged them into the ground, rolled out the sleeping bags and put them on top of the mats. It looked a bit empty and uninviting, she thought, so she walked along to the roadside and kicked around in the grass until she found a discarded bottle. Perfect. Lizzie snapped the stems of a few lupins and a couple of ferns and threaded them into the neck of the bottle before placing the arrangement in the corner of the tent.

Much better.

Bobby, assembling stones for a fire pit, grinned to himself. Lizzie was going to be just fine camping: she'd already made a flimsy bit of canvas into a little home.

Together they gathered sticks for the fire and he

created a little nest to balance the pans they filled with water from the river.

"Sunday roast or... chili?" he asked, reading the labels.

"Seriously?"

"Seriously. It's stuff the military uses. Great for camping. Just boil it up and there you go, dinner is served."

"It sounds disgusting..." she said dubiously.

"Well, you get used to it."

Lizzie, poking her fork into the warmed-up congealed mess in the bottom of the bag, didn't think she'd ever get used to it. She didn't even know if she'd had the chili or the roast. Two squashed slices of Mrs. Bingle's cake later, they climbed into their sleeping bags and Bobby zipped the doors shut. He had to unzip them five minutes later when Lizzie insisted on getting out and brushing her teeth, then grumpily followed her when she informed him there was no way she was sleeping in a tent with a boy who didn't clean his teeth.

"Bossy boots" he muttered under his breath.

That night, Lizzie had the dream of her mother again. Only this time, two other women stood beside her mother. They each looked a little older and Lizzie recognized Marion, her great-grandmother. The other must be her grandmother. The three women stood and beckoned Lizzie towards them – and this time, the river was a little less rocky, it was a little less wild. She still couldn't cross it, but it definitely looked safer.

The dream was one of those she didn't want to leave and she tried as hard as she could to fight against waking, pulling herself back to the river's edge for one last look at her family.

But someone else was calling her.

"Lizzie... Lizzie... LIZZIE!"

Bobby was all cheerful. "I know you look like Sleeping Beauty and all that, but we've got places to be. It's nine already. Get up before I pack you away in the tent!"

She'd slept for nearly twelve hours? She'd never done that.

"I think mother's happy I'm going there," she told Bobby. "And Marion, too. They're all happy. We're doing the right thing."

He had no idea what she was on about but would have agreed to anything if it meant she got up and they could start moving. He splashed cold water on her face.

"Oy! I'm moving!" She slithered out of the sleeping bag and said goodbye to the lupins as she threw them into the undergrowth.

"You know lupins mean happiness, right?"

Bobby knew about flowers?

He nodded. "Yup, lupins mean happiness. You, my friend, just threw out happiness."

"Really?"

"Mmhmm. But don't worry. Happiness also comes in chocolate bars. And lucky for you, I've got some."

Lizzie laughed and took the chocolate, munching away as she helped fold up the tent and kick the stones away they'd used for the fire pit.

"Take nothing but pictures, leave nothing but footprints," he told her. "Campers' charter."

"Where do canoes belong in the Campers' Charter?" she asked.

"There was a little frog going to a race. He was very small but had a big heart."

"What?"

"I'm telling you a story. About a frog."

Lizzie went back to squashing clothes into her backpack.

"So anyway, there's this frog. And he's at the

race. And when he got there, someone shouted at him that he was really small and he couldn't race. But the little frog didn't care, you know? He wanted to race, so he did."

"Bobby, is this the story of the hare and the tortoise only with a frog?"

"Listen!"

She mimed zipping her lips.

"Thank you. So. The frog went and raced, and every time the big frogs stopped because they were tired, he went past them. He won the race."

Lizzie was about to speak, lining up a triumphant, 'I told you so!' when Bobby held his hand up to stop her.

"Wait for the end! After the race, everyone wondered how he'd done it. Especially since they'd spent the whole race saying he was too small and why was he even trying. Turns out the frog was deaf and he didn't hear them telling him it was impossible."

There was silence.

"What on earth," said Lizzie eventually, "does that have to do with anything?"

"Nothing really. It's an Ojibwe story I read. I thought you'd like it."

Lizzie looked at him curiously, picked up her

backpack and started walking up towards the road.

"You know you're odd, right?" she said to him.

Bobby was just relieved. He'd made her forget about the canoe, hadn't he?

CHAPTER 10

PLAYING WITH FIREWEED

As the bus pulled into Kenora, Lizzie felt strange.

"I think I've been here before," she whispered to Bobby.

"You can't have been, you've never left the States before yesterday! Maybe it's deja vu? That thing you get when you feel like you're re-living, but you aren't really. It's just your brain working weirdly."

Lizzie was unconvinced. Maybe she'd explained it badly. It wasn't that she'd ever stood in front of that bus station before or looked at that row of shops or walked along that long curving walkway by the lake. It just felt familiar in a way that was right, as if she belonged.

"It's like I've come home," she said quietly.

"It's like you've gone mad," he said back. "More

important, I'm hungry. Let's eat."

Lizzie winced a little, hurt by him brushing off her feelings like that, but she followed him into the store and watched as he gathered up supplies.

"Bikes," Bobby said firmly as they came out.

"Yup, bikes," she agreed.

It was the only way for them to get to the lodge. Bobby had read about an abandoned logging road – that was going to be fun to bike... – that they'd need to find after they'd reached Grassy Narrows on a paved road, and he'd marked on a map where he thought it must go. Lizzie figured she'd trusted him so far, now would be a bad time to stop. Now that they were so close. Well, just under seventy miles.

Bobby reckoned it would take two days for them to get there so they rented the bikes for four days. Lizzie insisted on a red bike, just like the one she had at home. She loved the big wicker basket on the front and the shiny silver bell that gave a satisfying 'tring tring'.

"That'll help keep the bears away," Bobby said.

Lizzie looked horrified. "There's bears here?"

"I was just joking," Bobby lied. "Honestly, cross my heart, no bears. They've all gone north."

It sounded like he knew what he was talking

about so Lizzie believed him. She climbed onto the bike and wobbled out of the parking lot: it turned out cycling while wearing a heavy backpack wasn't that easy.

Bobby set off at a steady pace and soon realized he was leaving Lizzie behind.

"You go in front. It's your adventure, after all. Your great-grandparents' lodge," he told her. That protective thing coming in again. Lizzie's face was set in concentration as she wobbled slowly past him and set off into the shadows of the trees.

The path wound around endless miniature lakes. Close to Kenora, Lizzie saw families playing in the water: children shrieking as they leapt from a giant inflatable unicorn, mothers slapping sunscreen onto wriggling toddlers, fathers kicking balls and letting their sons win races to reach the ball first.

Lizzie remembered how Dad used to play with her when she was very small, how she'd spent hours in the little trailer behind his bike before she'd finally learned to balance a bike herself and, pedaling furiously, could just about keep up with him. She remembered making forts with him in the winter, cushions and blankets piled chaotically around the den, and Mrs. Dabble coming in and 'tut-tutting' her way through putting everything back in their rightful places.

Then Lizzie had started school and Dad could be away more, and he'd started going back to the office. His days became longer and longer and she saw him less and less. He became wrapped up in documents and angry phone calls, leaving the house before the sun came up and getting home after dark. Lizzie would often be woken by the sound of his feet scrunching across the gravel and she'd watch him place his briefcase on the back seat, hang a suit jacket over the passenger headrest, then get into the car and drive off.

She didn't like to go to sleep until she knew he was back home safe. Sometimes, she would sit and play cards for hours just to stay awake. With a teddy propped up on the pillows, Lizzie would sit on the bed and deal the cards for gin rummy. One for teddy, one for her, one for teddy, one for her...

She could shuffle a deck like a magician now, expertly flicking the cards up and down in her hands, creating and collapsing a bridge in the briefest moment.

The delighted shrieks of children grew quieter as they cycled further and further from Kenora. The greater distance between them and the town, the more wildlife Lizzie saw. Dappled loons bobbed in the little lakes, and an eagle shrieking high above cast a shadow that swooped across the grass. When they finally stopped for the evening alongside a place Bobby said was called Silver Lake, Lizzie sat and watched turtles float idly in the shallows, warming their shells and bodies in the last of the sunshine.

It was the perfect place for camping and Lizzie, having watched Bobby the day before, knew what to do. She helped stretch the canvas, feed in the poles, and held the pegs as once more he hammered them into the ground. They gathered stones for their fire pit, Bobby jokingly picking up a turtle to add to the circle, and Lizzie wrestled him into the water to release the relieved animal who flapped his flippers as hard as he could to get to safety.

She saw some lupins and then thought better of it – no more casually throwing happiness by the way side this time. Tall, pink flowers grew along the shore and she gathered stems of these together and took them over to Bobby.

"Go on then, what do these mean," she challenged him.

"That's fireweed."

"You're making it up. How do you know that?"

"Look, it's fireweed. Mom's really into this stuff. It's the only thing she likes about camping. Showing us all the flowers. It's called fireweed because it grows really easily where there's been fires. Oh, and it's a symbol of new stuff. Like, new things are going to happen."

Lizzie smiled happily and wrapped some long reeds around her bouquet to keep it together; no bottle-from-a-ditch this time. She propped them in the corner of the tent and handed Bobby the silver packets of boil-in-a-bag dinner.

"It says 'chili'. I'm unconvinced." She handed it over and he popped them into the pot.

Lizzie's hands hurt from gripping the handlebars and her shoulders ached from where the backpack pulled. The seat wasn't too comfortable, either, and neither was Bobby's judging by the way he casually leaned against a tree to eat his dinner rather than sitting alongside her in the grass.

That night, as Bobby lay awake and listened for the rustle of bears, Lizzie dreamed the same dream. Only this time, the three women were on the other side of a stream, and she could hear them calling.

If you say something in a convincing way, turns out people will often believe you.

CHAPTER 11

SUMS ON THE PORCH

It was already getting dark as they arrived at the lodge the following evening and, much as she wanted to explore, Bobby convinced her just to get into the tent and have some sleep. They'd had to sneak past the houses of Grassy Narrows – a touch difficult with two creaking bikes and endless sticks to be snapped underfoot. Lizzie wanted to meet the people who lived there, but not yet.

"First, the lodge," she'd insisted. So that is what they'd done. She'd kicked up a fuss when he pointed out that going to Whitedog wasn't an option, at least not on this trip, so he was letting her get her way with everything else to keep her happy.

Bobby wasn't too surprised when he woke to find her missing.

It had been impossible for Lizzie to sleep. She

was there, she was finally there! As soon as the canvas above her turned a shade lighter with the rising of the sun, she quietly slipped out of her sleeping bag, eased the zip of the tent doors open, and stepped out to discover the place that had made her great-grandparents so happy for so many years.

Lizzie looked and imagined the dock was still there, and she could almost see Barney standing next to one of his float planes, a cigar and a smile in place. The figure of Marion seemed to stand at the end of the dock, waving and welcoming her just as she had every guest who arrived at the lodge all those years ago. Looking along the lake shore, she could almost reach out and touch that endless line of perfectly placed boats, guides walking away into the evening sun.

The log cabins, long neglected, had caved in roofs and broken verandahs, but Lizzie hardly saw the damage. She walked into what must have been the main lodge and caught her breath: a Tiffany-style lamp still hung near the window, the early morning light splashing red and green and blue jewels across the dusty floorboards. A map of the English Wabigoon river system still hung on a wall, yellowing now but Lizzie could almost see the guests gathered in front of it, their fingers tracing the day's routes and the places they had caught the largest fish.

The kitchens were all but collapsed but all Lizzie could see was a line of perfect, gleaming stoves. Cans stacked regimentally on the shelves, order and precision, and there was Marion, sitting on her stool and ready with her ever-present white dishcloth, keeping track of every plate and wiping it clean of drips before allowing it to be presented to a diner.

A stuffed moose stood in one corner of the Great Room and Lizzie recognized it as Crazy Legs. He and her grandmother had taken their first wobbling steps together on the front porch; they grew up together, until Crazy Legs accidentally sat on the toddler one day and was forever dispatched to the corner of the room, unseeing eyes staring fixedly into nothingness.

Lizzie didn't see the cobwebs or the dust, didn't notice the beams that had rotted through and were sagging to the brink of breaking. To her, the place was still Barney's. It was filled with the tall tales and laughter of the wealthy fishermen who had come back year after year. Lizzie caught her breath to think of them all standing in that very room, sharing stories with her great-grandfather about the one that got away.

Heading along a meandering path she found a cabin with chairs still on the verandah, as if they were waiting for someone to come back from fishing. The chairs faced the perfect view across the calm, blue lake dotted with tiny islands. It was odd to think that something so beautiful held so much danger.

And that is where Bobby discovered her, leaning back on a worn out chair on a worn out porch, diving into memories that her great-grandmother had shared in the diaries found stowed away in the boxes they'd read through. It seemed impossible that anything bad could have happened here, that the lake wasn't safe, that the fish that jumped and created ripples could be bad for you.

"Eggs," Bobby said abruptly. "And cocoa. And –" he reached into his back pocket and triumphantly pulled out a pack of cards – "time for gin rummy, I think."

She looked surprised.

"Hey, I read Marion's diaries too, remember," he reminded her.

So they sat there, just as Lizzie imagined Barney and Marion had fifty years before, Bobby taking on Barney's role of making breakfast and then hands of gin rummy in perfect, companionable silence.

"It's funny," said Lizzie. "I've never played rummy with anyone before. Mrs. Dabble taught me years ago, but she never had time to play. I'm glad it was here, though. I'm glad it was with you."

Bobby gave up fighting the reddening in his cheeks.

"Thank you," she said. "Thank you for bringing me here. Whatever else happens, this is the best day of my life."

"Promised I would, didn't I?"

She picked up the cards and started to shuffle them.

"Damn! One more thing." He jumped up and hurried down the steps to the tent, returning with yesterday's bunch of fireweed. "*Now* it's perfect," he said as he placed the flowers on the table between them.

Lizzie leaned back in her chair and sighed. Contented. The sun was warm, a woodpecker had set to work attempting to decimate a nearby tree, and every now and then a fish flickered across the surface of the water. She walked down to the tent and returned bearing a pile of papers.

"You've carried those all this way? No wonder your bag weighs so much!" Bobby poked her in the ribs as she passed him.

"I'm here to work, too, remember," she told him.

"Why didn't you just take photos with your phone?"

Lizzie gave him a withering look. "Bobby, have you ever seen me with a phone?"

He had to concede he had not.

"I don't have one. Dad says I can learn everything I want to know from books, or by asking him. Only he's not around much, so it's just books for me. He doesn't want me messing around on the internet reading silly ideas about things. Okay? Right. Mercury. I want stats." She spoke sharply to cover her embarrassment.

"Stats?"

"Statistics." She looked across at him. "You know what statistics are, right?"

"Oh, sure!" he said airily. "Course I do."

"Look, they're numbers and charts and things. When you get a whole load of information about a place and can put it into numbers, you can get statistics. Stats." She shrugged awkwardly. "I like math, okay?"

Bobby pulled out one of the charts and skimmed across it.

"Go on then, explain this to me," he challenged.

Lizzie looked at the numbers and screwed up her eyes in concentration. One line told her that the Ontario government had put in place a figure of 0.5ppm – "I think that's 'parts per million'" she told Bobby – for safe levels of mercury in fish. But the fish in the Wabigoon and English river chain, and here in Ball Lake, had readings of up to 15ppm.

Bobby chipped in – he was reading through papers too. "That makes sense. Listen to this, it's from a letter by the guy who was the Health Minister. In 1972 he wrote that the levels of mercury in the fish are 'thirty times the maximum allowable limit set for mercury in fish, therefore fish from these waters should not be eaten.' And listen, here's another one. In 1975, they wrote, 'the conditions do not differ significantly from the situation that caused the tragedy at Minamata.'"

Lizzie pulled her head away from the charts for a moment. "So you're saying that what happened at Minamata has basically happened here? And they knew this all that time ago?"

The two looked at each other. The further they dived into the information, the worse it got. The only good thing that had happened around here was that

Barney closed because he didn't want the guides or guests to get sick.

The realization of what had been allowed to happen was making more and more sense. Lizzie replayed it all in her mind: the mill dumping mercury into the river, the government ordering them to stop in 1970, the mill *still* dumping ton after ton of mercury in the years that followed – and fighting, arguing, saying they were doing nothing wrong, that it wasn't dangerous. And all the time, the people of Grassy Narrows getting more and more sick, losing more and more of their life and way of living. When Barney ran his lodge, eight out of ten people from Grassy worked there. So when he closed, overnight eight out of ten suddenly didn't have a job – and nobody cared but Barney.

"But look," said Bobby. "The mill did give some money. See? In 1985. They gave $17.4million, to be exact. That's when the Ojibwe got the lodge, and your great-grandparents got a million dollars."

"And they were supposed to be grateful?" sneered Lizzie. "In fifteen years, my great-grandparents spent more than that on scientists and tests and –"

"I mean, it sounds like a lot to me, maybe not for Barney and Marion but for …". Bobby trailed off and felt her glare.

"It's simple sums," snapped Lizzie. "Right, I don't know all the figures, but we're talking fifty years since anyone found out about the mercury. Yes? 1970 they found it out. So okay, fifty years. Let's take 17.4 million and divide it by fifty…". To be honest, she regretted this at the moment but was going to keep on and prove her point. She leapt up and grabbed a stick to do the math in the dirt. "I'll make it easier. One million, seven hundred and fifty thousand divided by fifty is… three hundred and fifty thousand."

"Okay, so that's three hundred and fifty thousand a year. Still not bad!" Bobby looked at her and immediately wished he'd said nothing.

"Right. But look, there's over fifteen hundred people in Grassy Narrows today. And that money also went to the other people at Whitedog. So we're talking at least a few thousand people. I'll make my sums easy again and say two thousand, so that is the grand sum of a hundred and seventy five dollars a year for having your life ruined by mercury."

Bobby was starting to regret saying it was a lot of money. It really wasn't.

Lizzie carried on, she was on a roll.

"A hundred and seventy five dollars a year to say 'sorry' that any kids you have will be born with mercury poisoning. That's a hundred and seventy five dollars a year to say 'sorry', you probably won't be able to see or hear as well as other people. That's a hundred and seventy five dollars a year to say 'sorry', you might not be able to feel your hands and feet as you get older. And that's a hundred and seventy five dollars a year to say 'sorry', you could spill half of what you try and drink because your hands might be shaking so much."

She was almost shouting now, waving her hands higher and higher in the air with every statement.

She sat back in the chair, exhausted.

"It's not right, is it," said Bobby quietly.

"No," she agreed simply. "It's not."

CHAPTER 12

BACK HOME...

It's easy to forget the rest of the world when you're wrapped up in an adventure. Neither Lizzie nor Bobby had spared a thought for anyone back home. They were just intent on getting to their destination – and really, they were still only halfway there. Seeing the lodge was important but meeting the people of Grassy Narrows was just as important. The whole point had been to come and see the lakes and rivers, and find those who had been affected by the mercury poisoning.

But back home, Lizzie's father was becoming increasingly confused.

"Where did you say she'd gone, Mrs. Dabble?"

"I didn't. She just said she was going camping with the Bingle lad, Bobby. They're in the same class at school."

He frowned.

Mrs. Dabble stood her ground. "I told her to ask you about it."

"I've never heard her mention him, or any camping trip. Wait, she said something about a 'Bobby' the other day. I think. I don't know."

Mrs. Dabble kept her thoughts to herself on that one. She knew full well that Lizzie and her father never really talked about anything much. Her father, God bless him, didn't even buy her clothes the right size, never mind know who she spent time with at school.

"Still, I'll pop round and see the Bingles later. You couldn't rustle up one of your fabulous cakes for me to take over, could you Mrs. Dabble?"

It didn't take much to flatter Mrs. Dabble and she bustled off happily to the kitchen to busy herself with flour and eggs.

That evening, Lizzie's father presented himself at the Bingles, cake in hand and smile on his face.

"Edward! So nice to see you! It's been – well, it's been a long time, hasn't it?" Mr. Bingle grabbed his hand and pulled him inside, mentally calculating it was a good eight years or so since Edward had been round to the farm. "Cake? Fantastic. Sheila will sort that out. Sheila! It's Edward!"

Sheila came bustling in, slipping her apron off and heading straight for the drinks cabinet.

"Edward, it's been too long. Just too long. [Turning to her husband.] Don't I always say that, dear? [Turning back to Edward.] Too long. You must come over any time, you know. Especially since your Lizzie has been spending time with our Bobby. She's lovely, isn't she? So serious sometimes. I'm sure she does well at school. Am I right, or am I right? Beer, yes?"

It wasn't a question, really, as she thrust a glass into his hand as she asked it. Hands brushing against his shoulders, Sheila guided him into a chair and his feet were upon a footstool before he knew what had happened.

"When are you due, Sheila? Three not enough trouble for you?"

She smiled and rested her hand on her stomach. "Just a few weeks to go. This one's a girl; I just know it."

Her husband, Paul, covered his smile. She'd said that the last three times, too, and look where that had gotten them. Three boys who never stopped eating.

Edward sensed the possibility of a major diversion and shifted the conversation back to where he really wanted it to be. "I just wondered where Lizzie was, actually. Starting to worry a little, I guess. Apparently she went camping with Bobby? She's never been camping before."

"Oh yes!" Sheila clapped her hands. "They went yesterday, didn't they dear? I'm sure it was yesterday. And they'll be back tomorrow. I'm sure they said just two nights. Isn't that right?"

Paul shook his head.

"They went last week, Sheila. Let's see, it must be... five days ago now. Yes, that's right. Wait, you said they were only going for two nights?"

Edward and Sheila both stared at him.

It was Sheila who broke the silence.

"And you didn't say anything?"

"Well, what was there to say? The boy's been camping enough times before. I didn't know they were only going for two days, did I?"

Sheila was, by and large, an organized, practical sort of woman. She was a farmer's wife, after all, and there's no space to be squeamish or chaotic when you're a farmer's wife. But in that moment she was a mother first and foremost and her immediate reaction was to plump herself onto the sofa and burst into tears.

Paul looked apologetically at Edward before heading over to awkwardly pat his shaking jelly of a wife and say, "There, there."

"Look," said Edward, trying to get things organized in his mind. "Where did you say they were going camping?"

"Just over by the far side of the woods!" She let out a squeak.

"So let's head over there and see what they're up to."

A thorough inspection of the area revealed no sign of Lizzie or Bobby, and no suggestion that a tent had been pitched anywhere nearby either.

"That," said Paul proudly, "is because I showed him right. Take nothing but pictures, leave nothing but footprints. Look at the lad, he's tidied up after himself real good."

"Or they were never here," Edward said quietly.

Which set Sheila off again into a shower of squeaks and snuffles. It was a good five minutes before they could work out that she was saying something about the old barn.

Edward and Paul left her to her strange noises and walked outside. The farmer held a large lantern aloft and moths flickered and floated in and out of the light. As he opened the doors both men were speechless, looking at the neat rows of papers piled onto hay bales, the maps stuck on the walls, the chalkboard covered in circles and arrows and names.

"What the…?" Edward walked over and started picking up the papers. The highlighters Lizzie and Bobby had used made it easy: Barney Lamm, Marion Lamm, Grassy Narrows, mercury. That was the theme.

Paul was looking at the map and the red string Bobby had pinned in place.

"Er, Edward… You might want to see this."

Edward knew where they'd gone before he even looked at the map. "It's Barney's. Ball Lake Lodge. It belonged to Rachel's grandparents. Lizzie's doing a school project and I told her to check the boxes in the attic. I guess that's where all this" – he gesticulated towards the meticulous piles of paper clipped pages – "came from."

"What on God's earth is at Ball Lake Lodge?"

"It is… was… a hunting and fishing lodge. Said to be the finest in the whole of Ontario, if not Canada. They had to close it down in the 70s because of mercury pollution in the lake and river system. Huge scandal. Barney and Marion spent years fighting the government. I – I don't know what ended up happening. I've seen stuff about court cases over the years but I've been a bit, well, distracted I guess."

"You've been so distracted you didn't notice your daughter missing for five days straight?"

"In fairness, you didn't notice Bobby had gone either…". He shrugged. "Unhelpful. Right. Let's think about this. They can't have gone there. It's in Canada, and Lizzie doesn't have a passport."

"You don't know my son…" said Paul, grimly. "He's a determined little sod. Once he gets an idea in his head, he'll work out a way you mark my words. Might not be the right way, but it'll be a way."

Edward turned pale. "I think it's all my fault."

Paul looked at him. "What?"

"Yes… She was asking about mercury poisoning the other day. I told her she should speak to someone with mercury poisoning, then she'd understand it. I'd like to bet she took that as an instruction to go and meet these people up by the lake."

"What people?" stormed Paul.

"The ones who were poisoned! The lodges up there all employed guides who took the guests out fishing. When the lake was found to be polluted – it was a paper mill or something" – Paul pointed to the word 'Dryden' on the chalkboard – "yup, that's the one. Dryden. They just dumped tons of mercury into the river system for years, and it got into the fish. I think it was Grassy Narrows" – Paul hit his finger against 'Grassy Narrows' on the chalkboard and nodded – "where most of the guides came from. The mill just denied everything for years and the government passed the buck for decades. Nobody wanted to admit anybody had done something wrong. Meanwhile, the people at Grassy Narrows carried on eating the fish; what else were they supposed to eat? Many got seriously sick. Pregnant women even ate it, you know. It's awful. All that mercury passes over to the baby inside them. Kids were being born, poisoned, before they'd drawn their first breath."

"And you're telling me that your daughter has gone on, what, a crusade or something with my son? She's dragged my son into this?" Paul's anger was filled with fear. He thought of Sheila and their unborn child, and he couldn't bear to reach further into his mind and wonder how it must feel for these women Edward spoke of, knowing they were poisoning their own children as they grew inside them.

"I don't know. I still don't know how they could even get there. I mean, I guess it's possible."

Edward's face was tight. He pushed the words out through his teeth.

"So what do you propose doing now? Bake another cake and wait for them to come back?"

Edward thought for a moment. He thought of the court case – Irene Ward was due in court tomorrow. She needed him. But he needed his daughter. He desperately tried to push back the images that rushed into his mind. Anything could have happened to her. Anything.

A photo stuck on the wall caught his eye. Barney Lamm, grinning with a cigar and a sea plane. Edward's mind leapt towards a crazy idea.

"Look, I'll take the plane. I'll go up there tomorrow."

Paul's eyes followed Edward's and landed on the picture. "That old thing? That plane you've been storing in my hangar all these years? That's a relic! You can't fly that!"

Edward looked at him. "Got a better idea?"

Paul looked at the map, looked back at Edward, roared as loudly as he could, and then stormed off in the direction of the hangar.

"We'd best get working on her, then. You can go first thing tomorrow."

CHAPTER 13

THE WORLD GOES DARK

"We're saved!"

Lizzie turned and watched Bobby as he ran down towards the little beach.

"I didn't know we needed saving? And what's that you're holding?"

Bobby showed her two cans, still sealed. "I found them where the kitchen used to be. Guess they left something behind. Anyway, stuff doesn't go bad in cans. I sort of didn't mention it, but we're running low on food. Oh – check these out." Bobby handed over his baseball cap, filled with bright red jewel-like berries. "They're chokecherries."

"They're red. Doesn't that mean 'danger'? And what do you mean, we're sort of low on food?"

"I get hungry. I eat. It happens. Anyway, there's a

load of cans up in the old kitchen so if we can just figure out how to open them, we're good to go for a while. And these berries. Trust me, the Ojibwe eat them. I read about it."

Lizzie wasn't convinced by either the cans or the chokecherries – the name was enough to put her off for a start. The last time Marion and Barney had been at the lodge was back in November 1985. Even if the cans were brand new then, that still made them over thirty years old.

She compromised. If there were more cans, they'd at least eat from the ones that looked the least beaten up. And she told herself that maybe the people of Grassy Narrows had left them after giving up trying to run the lodge; that would make the cans fractionally less ancient.

There was quite a stash: a shelf seemed to have fallen, and Lizzie's heart hurt a little for Marion and her orderly lines of cans. "English names to the front" is how she'd liked it, a row of "little peas" and not "petit pois" she'd written, amused at herself, in her diary. All the labels had long since gone so they just picked the cleanest cans without any dents and took those down to the water's edge. Hammering with a stone didn't get them far and Bobby wasn't going to risk blunting his penknife (which was, along with a pebble he'd found in the shape of a dolphin, his most prized possession) so he went back on a treasure hunt and emerged triumphant from a cabin with a screwdriver in hand.

The first can contained Spam. The second, spaghetti.

"I guess that's the starter and the main course," said Bobby cheerfully. "And the chokecherries, of course, for dessert."

"You can keep those, I'll stick with the thirty year old spaghetti thanks very much."

"Suit yourself. More for me!"

They sat by the lake, Bobby sucking the chokecherries between his teeth, getting every ounce of juice he could from the pits before, pah!, spitting the stone out into the lake.

"They're kind of bitter but they're okay. Sure you won't try one?"

Lizzie shook her head. She left him to it, heading back up to the cabin where the two chairs sat quietly looking at the view and her bunch of bright pink fireweed made it complete. She stayed there watching the sunset, all the while imagining how Marion had maybe sat right here, right in this chair, and watched that same view. It hadn't changed in years. Maybe the trees were a little taller, and there was no plane and no line of boats along the shore, but if she tried really hard she could imagine it…

Lizzie woke with a start. She saw dark shadows on the lake, heard the gentle *thunk* of wood against wood then saw a silhouette emerge from a boat. The silhouette was pacing towards the tent and then it bent down and picked up – it picked up Bobby! Lizzie let out a tiny gasp.

Bobby hung limply in the silhouette's arms, his head lolling backwards and arms falling towards the ground. The silhouette staggered a little and went back to the boat, placing Bobby inside. Then the silhouette turned and headed back into the camp.

Was it looking for her? Lizzie looked wildly around but there was no time to go anywhere. The only place was into the cabin behind her. She slid as quietly as she could from the chair and prayed the floorboards wouldn't creak as she slipped into the dark room and held her breath, listening to her heartbeat echoing out into the still night.

She saw the silhouette approaching, heard him climb the few steps to the porch, and saw as he raised the fireweed from the table. Now he'd know for sure she was there.

Just as Lizzie was about to try and make a run for it after all the floorboard beneath her gave a final creak and groan then gave way. She shrieked as she fell, grasping at thin air and banging her head against the door frame. In the final moments before she passed out, she saw the silhouette come towards her and bend to pick her up.

CHAPTER 14

LIFT OFF

Edward and Paul worked all night on the ancient Piper. They wheeled it down to the lake, carefully steering the plane on its dolly and avoiding the rockier patches of ground.

"Sure there's enough room for take-off here?" asked Paul doubtfully, eyeing up his lake.

"There has to be," Edward replied through gritted teeth. "Hand me that oil again, would you?"

The plane had been in storage for the best part of twenty years. Rachel had inherited it from her grandfather when nobody else in the family seemed interested. Edward had learned to fly years before with an uncle, so it made sense that she – they – should have the plane. But life had gotten in the way and they didn't have time for those adventures, and then Rachel had died and Edward couldn't bear to have anything to do with the thing.

He'd never even told Lizzie about it.

He was fighting an inner battle. Part of him was incredibly proud of Lizzie for heading up to the wilderness with Bobby. 'Just like her mother,' he muttered to himself. That same determined, stubborn streak that had run through the family. He'd seen the photos of Marion once before and had chuckled: that family really did have strong genes and Rachel had inherited every last one of them. He was beginning to see it in Lizzie, too.

And look at the research she'd done! Lizzie had been meticulous, with her color coordinated sticky notes and everything set up in perfect order.

But most of him was just worried. Terrified, even, but this mission had no room for terror. Flying was the easy part, like riding a bicycle. And the lake *would* be long enough for a take off; he *would* find Lizzie and Bobby, and he *would* bring them home.

He would hug Lizzie again. They would be together again. They were a team. In that moment when he'd realized where she'd gone, he had seen what she was able to do without him – and how little he was without her.

Stinking of gasoline and dripping with sweat,

Paul declared victory.

"If she doesn't start now, she never will."

They maneuvered the plane onto the water and Edward carefully climbed aboard. It had been years since he'd sat in a plane and he'd never flown this one but it all came back to him. He flicked the switches.

This throttle... forwards.

This one... backwards.

Dials started to spin into action. It seemed to be working.

Press here... pull that lever... Cranked by Bobby's dad, the propeller started spinning, slowly at first but quickly picking up speed until it was nothing but a faint blur on the end of the Piper's nose. He eased the plane towards the most distant corner of the lake and turned it so that the longest clear patch of water stretched in front of him.

"Okay, let's get this old girl back up in the air." He crossed his heart, looked to the sky, then stifled an inner scream as he finally let her push her way across the lake.

The trees on the distant shore grew larger by the moment. If he didn't take off before he got there... It wasn't an option. He watched as the dials showed the Piper picking up speed... faster, he needed it to go faster…

The little plane in turn screamed at him, and just when he couldn't bear it a moment longer he pulled back the stick and they lifted from the water and up, up over the trees. Up over the farm. Up over the town with tiny people pointing and waving. He turned sharply to the north and settled in for the flight. He'd worked out it would be around five hours. Lunchtime. He could be there by lunchtime.

CHAPTER 15

THE FIRST MEETING

Far away in her dream, for the first time Lizzie saw a little bridge leading over the stream. Within moments she was across it, wrapped in the arms of all three women, each of them pressing her close and reassuring her that she was 'safe, you're safe now, Lizzie'.

She woke and found herself half buried under a pile of thick blankets. She was lying on her back and could hear water lapping. Jerking herself upright, her head throbbed.

She was in a boat, on a lake, in the middle of nowhere.

Turning round she saw the silhouette – a man. He smiled at her, held a finger to his lips and gestured for her to lie down again. He killed the engine and pulled out a paddle, moving it slowly and rhythmically through the water so the boat glided towards the dock where she could see more people waiting for them.

Bobby lay at the man's feet, also covered in blankets. His face was white as snow. Lizzie gasped but the man just nodded and smiled at her, patted Bobby's shoulder gently as if to reassure her.

The sun was creeping over the horizon and Lizzie felt its warmth on her face. The man was so calm, the world so very asleep and quiet, and her head hurt so badly she could do nothing but lie quietly and accept whatever was going to happen to them.

But she felt safe. Safer, perhaps, than she had in years. Safer than those dark evenings when she waited for the scrunch of Dad's car on the gravel to announce his arrival home.

Dark eyes smiled a welcome and gently, so gently, hands were placed under her elbows to help her up. The man stepped out and leaned in to gather up Bobby, safe in his blankets, and he carried him up towards a clearing. Lizzie followed.

Bobby was laid carefully in the center and a man came apart from the crowd and walked over to Lizzie.

"Matthew Keewatin," he said smiling, holding out his hand.

"Oh my," she stammered. Keewatin. That had

been the Chief's name when Barney had closed the lodge. "I mean hello. I mean mino gigizheb."

Everyone listening chuckled a little.

"And boozhoo to you. We just say 'boozhoo' here. Keep it casual. You speak Ojibwe?"

"Only a few words. You know, to be polite. Sorry, my head hurts a bit. I can't remember more than 'good morning' just now. Boozhoo. I'll try to remember that."

"That's alright. Your boy here" – he pointed at Bobby – "he ate chokecherries, am I right? And sucked on the stones?"

Lizzie's eyes widened. How did he know?

"He'll be fine. Just a bit sick for a while. Those stones, they contain cyanide. You aren't supposed to crunch them." And in response to her alarmed face, "Oh don't worry, he's only had the tiniest bit. He'll just be feeling sorry for himself in a few hours, nothing worse than that."

An old man in the crowd came forwards and limped up to her. He touched her arm, as if to check she was real. "She looks familiar," he said.

Other elderly people came out of the crowd. All of them did the same as the first: they reached out and touched her. One old lady put her fingers under

Lizzie's chin and turned her head gently to one side then the other.

"Yes, you do look familiar," she said.

"I'm Marion and Barney Lamm's great-granddaughter," Lizzie told them, feeling shy. "Marion Lamm? Yes, she was my great-grandmother. Apparently I look quite a bit like her. I'm Lizzie. I came here to see the Ball Lake. And the lodge. I read about everything that happened here and wanted to see it and learn about the mercury. And I wanted to meet the people my great-grandparents were such friends with."

A chair appeared from nowhere and Lizzie was pressed into it. A little girl with jet black hair came forwards, wide-eyed, encouraged by her mother, handing Lizzie a dandelion before rushing back to the safety of her mother's skirts.

"And is this Barney Lamm's great-grandson, then?" Matthew pointed towards Bobby.

"Oh no! No. He's just – just a friend. He helped me get here. He's Bobby. Nothing to do with Barney at all. Well, I mean, we did have a bit of an adventure getting here. And he made me breakfast, and we played gin rummy, and…". Lizzie trailed off.

"We knew you had come," said Matthew. His

voice was smooth and soft, calming and authoritative at the same time. "We knew you were coming yesterday, we heard the bikes rattling along the road. We don't miss much. I sent Isaac here to check on you" – the silhouette-then-a-man-now-Isaac nodded his head – "and it seems we came at the right time, what with your friend Bobby having fallen ill."

"Sorry I scared you," said Isaac.

"And your parents? Where are they?" Matthew asked.

"We sort of came on our own." Saying it out loud suddenly made it all the more real. Lizzie gave a bit of a laugh. "We came here on our own," she repeated slowly. She still couldn't quite believe it herself, with the last few days and everything they had done flashing through her mind.

Matthew smiled at her and spoke to the crowd. "Don't they sound just like Barney and Marion?!"

The crowd chuckled and nodded, all smiles and memories.

"You know your great-grandfather was inducted as an honorary Chief of the Grassy Narrows band?"

Lizzie's eyes widened.

"Yes, he was one of our friends. Had been for years. You know, Barney's a bit of a legend around these parts. When the mercury problem hit, he put his money where his mouth was and actually helped us out. Helped us find the truth. He closed the lodge because he thought it wasn't safe for us to be eating the fish."

"It was so sad," said one of the ladies. "My mom worked in the kitchens there; she lost her job when they had to close. When nobody else would help us, Barney and Marion fought. When politicians lied, they fought back. When the newspapers called him a traitor to the tourist industry, they kept fighting. So many people hated them for what they did. But not us."

"They had to leave Kenora, where they had their home," said another. "Chased out. Abandoned by their friends. Everyone tried to make them feel guilty for destroying the lodge business. But what could they do? They wanted to help us. They wanted to do what was right." The words were spoken with a quiet sorrow.

Lizzie felt their years of hurt. For fifty years they had lived with what had happened to them. For fifty years they had suffered.

"So did they win in the end? What happened?" Lizzie didn't know the end of the story. The papers in the boxes had stopped shortly after Barney's death in 2002.

Matthew spread his hand across the horizon.

"What do you see?" he asked Lizzie.

"I, I'm not sure... I guess I see a beautiful lake, and beautiful trees. That's good, isn't it?"

"You see a beautiful lake – and every living thing in it is still poisoned with mercury. You see beautiful trees – that the logging companies want to cut down."

"So my great-grandparents lost everything, and you did too?" Lizzie's shoulders slumped.

Matthew patted her arm gently. "Barney and Marion put their heart and soul into righting the mercury tragedy so they could re-open the lodge and help us. They gave everything they had. They fought for what is right and true. They gave us hope. And you" – he gently placed his fingers beneath her chin and tilted her head to look up at him, to be sure she understood what he was saying – "you coming all the way here to find us? You give us hope, too."

The crowd nodded silently.

CHAPTER 16

A SAFE PLACE

There's nothing like bright yellow projectile vomit to break an awkward moment. If Lizzie didn't know that already, she definitely did after Bobby suddenly sat bolt upright, pushed off his blankets, and sent a perfect fluorescent shower straight out in front of him. Some of the small children giggled and pointed.

Lizzie rushed over to him and banged him firmly on the back, just as Mrs. Dabble had done that time she'd been sick.

Bobby turned to shout at her, thought better of it, and instead sent out another yellow spray.

"Golly" was all he could muster.

Lizzie was so relieved that she forgot to be angry with him for eating the stones of the chokecherries, and she didn't care that some of the bright yellow pressed onto her grey dress as she hugged him. It was covered in mud and grass stains by now anyway; the yellow might even improve it.

A boy about their age walked forwards and shyly introduced himself as Joe. His great-grandfather, he said, had been the one to honor Barney Lamm by making him Chief Thunderbird Continuous Day. He and Lizzie exchanged looks, suddenly profoundly aware of the difference their ancestors had made in the world. They were connected by invisible threads through the decades, both in this awkward place of trying to work out how they belonged in the narrative.

Bobby felt terribly small and irrelevant all of a sudden. The stories these two had to look back on were so much better than his family's, he thought! The farm where he lived had been handed down from generation to generation, never really prospering but never failing either. They had quiet lives on the fringes of the world, never venturing further than was needed. The enormity of his and Lizzie's adventure suddenly sat as a weight on his shoulders. Without Lizzie and her determination, he would still be sitting on a wall throwing stones at tin cans, whiling away the hot days by chasing turtles in the lake and listening to the crickets announce the arrival of yet another warm afternoon.

"Come!" said Joe. "You must both stay here with us. Let's go get your things."

He led them to a canoe and helped Lizzie get in. Bobby winced a little seeing somebody else helping her, taking over his self-appointed role as Lizzie's protector. Bobby paddled as hard as he could, just to give a show of strength and remind Lizzie that he was there too; within a few hundred yards the sweat poured from his brow and he was panting, exhausted. Joe smiled from the stern of the wooden canoe, easing the boat across the small waves the wind was whipping up. They had nearly five miles to travel and the trick, he had learned, was to pace yourself.

"Take the boat!" his father had said as he saw Joe leading them to a canoe, but the boy had ignored him. The fumes and noise always gave him a headache and Joe far preferred to paddle – besides, as with everything in his life, there was no rush.

It didn't take long to gather their things together at the lodge, and Joe even managed to balance the bikes across the deck, lashing them down with lengths of cord to keep them safe. They were about to leave when Lizzie asked them to wait and, a little embarrassed and rushing so they couldn't see what she was doing, she grabbed a small package from a pocket in the backpack and ran back up the beach to the cabin where she had sat and played gin rummy with Bobby just the day before.

She needed to leave something to honor Barney and Marion, she thought, and pulled out the cigar she had stolen from Dad's desk and carried all the way. She gathered flowers and arranged them on the porch as well as she could, something for Marion to look down upon and smile.

And then, in the sand by the canoe, she took a stick and marked out the words, "Thank you for our safe place."

"What's that about?" Bobby pointed at the words.

"That book made me think of it. 'No Safe Place.' One of the books about everything that happened. I wanted Barney and Marion to know that even now, with everything that has happened here, the lodge is still a safe place. It was for us."

Bobby was about to say something teasing when Joe chimed in, "This land is our safe place, too. We're still fighting for it, but it's ours. Thank you," and Bobby was glad the words hadn't tumbled off his tongue.

Lizzie blushed a little and Joe once more helped her into the canoe, and once more Bobby felt a little dash of irritation. Once more he paddled badly – a little better, having watched Joe with half an eye to see how he achieved such a smooth, strong motion – and felt a pang of jealousy as he saw the two exchange smiles and point out birds. Joe talked to her about the fish, the pike and bass and walleye that rich Americans used to come here for.

Bobby had been relegated from Expedition Organizer to Chief Spare Part.

As they unloaded the bags and bikes back at Grassy Narrows, a strange buzzing sound started in the sky. Everyone stopped what they were doing to be able to focus and listen to this alien noise: there was no animal, no human, who could sound like that. The noise became louder and louder and a small yellow dot appeared in the distance.

"It's a plane!" somebody shouted. "And it's headed towards Barney's!"

Looks were exchanged, then everyone rushed down to the water to leap into the waiting boats, engines buzzing into life. This was no time for idle canoe trips and bird spotting. Lizzie and Joe jumped quickly into a boat and Bobby, rolling his eyes a little, thought 'here we go again' and threw himself in after them. Another chance to watch Joe take over. Just perfect.

CHAPTER 17

THE REUNION

Lizzie's father landed the little plane neatly enough, managing to hide the fact he hadn't flown for the past few decades. The propeller slowed as he glided towards the beach. Leaping from the floats, he dashed to turn the plane around, hauling it up onto the beach so it wouldn't drift away. Then he rushed towards the disintegrating lodge, calling his daughter's name again and again until his throat hurt.

Something caught his eye in front of one of the cabins, one where two chairs still stood and looked out towards the lake. He raced up the few steps to the porch and saw a cigar – just like those he had at home – and a bouquet of flowers, lovingly tied with long reeds and resting prettily on the table.

He was sure Lizzie had left those, it was the sort

of thing she'd do. But now there was no sign of his Lizzie or Bobby.

He walked back down towards the plane, dejected, exhausted, unsure what the next step should be. Something written in the sand caught his eye. 'Thank you for a safe place.' Whatever that meant, at least it was good. It wasn't an SOS or a desperate plea. As he stood there, helpless, unsure what to do next, it suddenly felt as if Rachel was right next to him. He reached out his hand and could almost sense hers in his, smell her perfume on the breeze.

Sounds travel easily across water and the boats from Grassy Narrows were still far away when he heard them approaching, shattering his perfect moment with his vision of Rachel and hauling him back into the present. People were shouting and calling to him and he ran to the beach and waved back. Maybe they had seen Lizzie?

Lizzie, sitting in one of the boats that was bouncing excitedly across the waves, squinted her eyes against the sunlight and checked again. It really did look like Dad, but what on earth would he be doing here? Joe pushed the engine hard, rushing the boat towards the beach. It *was* Dad!

Not really thinking, Lizzie leapt to her feet and

waved wildly and called out to him.

"Dad!"

"Lizzie!"

Surprise and relief and confusion mixed everything together and Lizzie waved as hard as she could.

"Lizzie, get down!" called Bobby – too late, as she tripped on a rope and fell into the lake with a shriek.

Absolute chaos erupted. Nobody was going to let Lizzie drown (nobody bothered to check if she could swim, either, which she could as it happens). Lizzie's father was the first in the water, Joe a close second and Bobby, cursing the speed of the other boy, jumped in third. Men and women from the other boats also leapt wildly into the water: nobody was going to drown on their watch.

It turned out that Lizzie really didn't need rescuing. In fact, she was a stronger swimmer than all of them, even with her huge dress ballooning around her like a giant grey jellyfish. Within a few minutes everyone was piled on the shore, the boats as neatly ordered as the fishing boats were back in Barney's day. They were a mass of wet bodies steaming gently as the sun drew the water from their clothes.

Lizzie and her father sat to one side, each a little

unsure what to say to the other. Both had revealed so many secrets in those few moments that it was as if they were meeting for the first time.

"Dad," she finally asked. "Where did you get that plane from?"

"I have so much to tell you, Busy Lizzie," he told her. "And you have to tell me everything, too. I don't know how you made it up here but it's incredible. What an adventure you two have had" – he nodded towards Bobby who was sitting awkwardly to the side, still feeling uninvolved in it all. "Hey Bobby! Come join us!"

The boy gratefully came over and sat down.

"Thank you for looking after my Lizzie."

"Oh, that's okay, Sir. She's not that much work," Bobby replied with a dig into Lizzie's ribs. "I say. You didn't bring any food with you did you?"

"Bobby!" yelled Lizzie. "You've only just wound up being sick!"

"So now I'm hungry again! What do you expect when there's nothing inside me?"

"Ridiculous boy," Lizzie muttered under her breath, quietly laughing to herself. All of this – the lake, the plane, the feeling of home, everyone lying on the shore drying off in the sunshine and waiting for them to come back and be their guests at Grassy – all of this would never have happened without Bobby Bingle.

They all headed to Grassy Narrows, the Piper secured on the shore and Lizzie's father added to the little boat. When the engine was switched off and lifted above the shallow water, Bobby instructed him in how to use the paddle as they approached the dock. Edward smiled and let the boy have his moment of importance.

Someone beckoned Lizzie over to help with preparing a meal for them all. A shore lunch, they told her. Just as it used to be when the lodge was running.

Fish, of course. But fish bought in Kenora, imported from a thousand miles away. Five women worked together in a long line, three separate fires covered in pots and pans that bubbled and breathed out scented promises of delicious food. And as the plates were filled, Lizzie took each one and checked it, wiping the sides neatly with a cloth where the sauce had strayed, checking each dish was perfect before it was served.

"Just like Marion," an old lady chuckled and patted Lizzie's cheek softly. "That's just how she did it, too. With the same look on her face. It's like looking into the past."

Thick slices of bacon appeared as an appetizer. Walleye followed with canned spaghetti and canned beans. Freshly cut onions were piled onto the plates. And everything was rounded off with thick slices of bread smothered in butter and strawberry jelly.

CHAPTER 18

HIGHS AND LOWS

Lizzie's father made sure Bobby was just as much a part of the place and the conversations, asking him questions about the corn and the cattle on his farm. The men and boys crowded around, impressed when Bobby talked about the time he'd helped his father deliver a calf by reaching in and tying a rope around the hooves while it was still inside its mother.

"And did that make you sick, too?" someone said, slapping him on the back, and they all broke into laughter. Bobby had to tell a puzzled Edward about the chokecherries and the bright yellow vomit, giving a vivid reenactment of the moment he 'came back to life' that had everyone in stitches.

Then the food was passed around and the stories were shared of Barney and Marion.

"Do you remember," somebody roared, "that he wanted to fly people to the North Pole for afternoon tea?"

Everyone laughed and laughed.

"He'd have done it too!" chimed in someone else. "That man would have done any foolish thing if he'd thought he could make a buck out of it!"

"And what about that time he loaded a baby bear cub into the luggage compartment of his friend's plane? Eric, wasn't it? He convinced Eric to do him a favor and fly the plane over the border to Minneapolis."

"Yes – and the customs guys found the bear, of course, and Eric was arrested! That took some explaining by Barney, for sure!"

Lizzie loved every moment. The stories grew taller and wilder by the moment. "And they're all true," her father whispered in her ear.

"Remember when he jumped out of the plane?" someone said and many nodded that yes, yes, they remembered that story too. "Wait – I have the article somewhere!" And he dashed off to return minutes later with a file bursting with pages. Peering across, Lizzie recognized some from those she'd found in the boxes.

"Listen to this. 'He says he had only one accident in his fifty years of flying. He bought a war surplus plane and was ferrying it home when ice formed on the wings and propellor over the Blue Mountains of North Carolina. The plane rapidly lost altitude. When he heard the wings hitting the treetops, he opened a door and jumped out. He walked four miles through the forest until he met some people who could help him.'"

Everyone cheered and clapped and raised their glasses to honor the madness and the bravery.

"Everyone came to Barney's," an elderly man said from the corner. "Anyone who was anyone came here. The politicians... the movie stars... the sports stars... we even had a famous Mafia boss come up and fish with us."

Lizzie and Bobby couldn't have been more wide eyed if they tried. All these people had come here? All of them had walked through those same log cabins they had poked their heads into? Maybe they had sat in the same chair as film stars. "Or as murderers," as Bobby darkly put it to his friends a few months later. "That Mafia guy...".

"They were amazing," one woman said softly. "Remember the year the prices we were offered for wild rice were so low? Barney bought all our harvest up at a higher price, forcing anyone else who wanted rice to pay more for it."

"My father took me as a kid to their house in Kenora one Christmas Day. We took them a rabbit, in case they wanted it for dinner. Marion invited us in, and we sat there in their fancy living room and had a drink with them."

"They were our friends," somebody said. Everyone nodded their heads.

"And they respected us," the first woman added. "The other camp owners – they used us. We know this land and these waters better than anyone. We know where the fish are biting when the wind blows from the east; we know when the fish go deep, and where the moose hide out in the marshes. People made a fortune out of what we know, and when there was a chance they'd lose that they just didn't care about us."

She paused, unable to continue speaking about something that still hurt so much. Matthew stood up and took over where she'd left off.

"Barney and Marion were different, that's what you need to know. They needed us as much as we needed them, and they knew it. We helped them build their lodge and their business. They didn't just use us. They were generous and kind and good people – right to the end. Even while they were losing their business, they didn't forget about us. Not like the others. Not like the others at all."

Lizzie slowly looked around the group, her eyes settling on individuals: the kind faces with eyes dressed with crows' feet.

And as she looked more closely, she started to notice the signs. What the mercury had done to these people who laughed and shared and loved together. She saw moments when their hands would shake and eyes that often flickered. She saw people leaning in to others to repeat the comments, speaking closely and clearly for those who could no longer hear as they once could. When people got up to walk over to the fire to refill their plates, some were unsteady, walking as if they were drunk when all they'd had was soda.

Lizzie asked about the fish now, fifty years later, and they told her that no, the fish still weren't safe to eat. That they wouldn't be safe to eat for maybe another sixty or seventy years, because that is how long it would take for the mercury to finally leave the system. She asked about the wild rice, and they told her that logging had flooded the areas where the wild rice had grown and now it hardly grew there anymore.

Bobby chipped in, a little sadly. "So... you no longer hunt? And you no longer trap?" (Bobby had done rather more research than even Lizzie expected.) "But isn't that your right?"

As the evening went on, the stories were fewer and those that were told were laced with the weight of sadness. People spoke of those who had died – and those who had walked away one evening and didn't return to their families and were never heard from again. Lizzie heard how the children learned not to go into Kenora if they could help it because it was full of rumors and spite and a cold, untempered malice. Some of the older people admitted they only went to town now when they had to visit a doctor. "It's not worth it," they shrugged, reluctant to remember everything they had endured.

Lizzie's father looked across at the group and saw a little tiredness come into their faces. They had been fighting for so long for their 'rights' and every day in a small way these rights were being taken away. Fifty years and they were still fighting. He saw grandparents who were passing down the things they remembered to their children and grandchildren, but each generation in turn was forgetting a little of the traditions. And so much of their time was spent just fighting for the right to live in peace, to keep the loggers away from their land, to have what had been promised to them well over a hundred years ago.

And his heart broke for them, and it broke for Lizzie. For so long he had protected her from the world, from the truth. He had wrapped her up in the safest place he knew, kept her in the middle of nowhere so nothing could happen to her and she didn't need to know of the violence and despair and hurt that punctuated so many lives. Yet here she was, learning it all in one sudden rush of knowledge. Learning that people who were once your friends can turn on you in a moment, the way Barney Lamm's fellow tourist operators had done when he closed down Ball Lake and started to tell the world about the mercury in the fish. Learning that money and power can change people in a heartbeat, and that goodness and kindness are so often hidden and buried.

He thought back to her words scratched in the sand, 'Thank you for a safe place', and he realized that he had kept from her the one thing she should have always known. And look at her, he thought: she belongs here. Her profile, lit by the flickering flames of a fire, showed that same set determination he had loved so much in her mother; it was the same strength he had seen in the pictures of Rachel's mother and grandmother, handed down through the generations to see the wrongs in the world and fight to right them.

And as he watched, he saw Bobby go to Lizzie and place a blanket over her shoulders, and he smiled to himself. This boy was growing up, too. They had learned more in that week than in the twelve years they had lived before, safe in their retreat far away from the cries of the 'real' world.

CHAPTER 19

THE PACT

S ome things can be solved easily – like returning a canoe that you've 'borrowed' to slip across from the States to Canada.

And other things – well, they aren't always so easily solved. Explaining to the Canadian authorities just why he had hopped over the border in a vintage plane with no passport and no flight plan took a little explaining by Lizzie's father.

Explaining to Lizzie that they did need to leave was another tricky one. Joe's sister, Anong, had made that extra tricky.

"Anong? It means 'star'. My mom chose it because I was born on a cloudy night when no other stars could be seen. But what I really wanted to tell you is about the blockade." And she talked about how, since 2002, people from Grassy had gone daily to ensure the logging trucks couldn't enter their reservation. After more than a decade they'd won the first stand-off but there were always other areas where the loggers tried to come into their territory and back they'd go, lying down in the road in silent protest to protect their land.

Lizzie was fierce when she said she wanted to stay and take her turn in the line.

But they left reluctantly the next day, with promises to return in a few weeks' time.

"Dad has an important case to finish up," explained Lizzie, feeling more than a little foolish for putting anything above the battles these people had been fighting for over half a century. "But he's said we can come back and camp again. Bobby, too."

They made plans to see each other. Joe and Anong would teach Lizzie and Bobby how to fish the way their ancestors had, even if they did have to throw the fish back into the lake afterwards. They would show them the patches where wild rice still grew, and if they came back late enough in August for the Wild Rice Moon they could learn to harvest it, knocking it into the open canoes with a stick. They would teach them the words of their language that was slipping through their fingers, a little more lost with each generation that passed. They would teach them about the clans – Sturgeon, Loon, Caribou, Lynx, Pelican and Moose – and how their world revolved around the spirits and the skies and the freedom that was being taken away, inch by inch.

And they would sit and talk about how everything had come to pass. How Barney and Marion had fallen in love with this place in the middle of nowhere, and how they had created the most extraordinary, legendary lodge from the trees that grew by the lake with the help of Joe and Anong's great-grandparents. They would talk of the days when the mill thrived and poured ton after ton of mercury into the cleanest, purest river in the world. And they could go and see it, too. They could visit Dryden and see the mill and the source of all this horror.

And life, for Lizzie and Bobby and Joe and Anong, would never quite be the same again. Because they had learned to look beyond their four walls and to find caring and kindness in people who didn't need to give it. Together, the four had forged a pact. Promises had been made that would never be broken. Plans were underway. The future would be different.

Before Lizzie left, Joe pressed a little wooden eagle into her hand.

"This means we'll always be with you," he promised her earnestly. "And what it means to us is everything that you are. Honesty, truth, and courage."

"Giga-waabamin menawaa," Lizzie had said carefully as she left. "See you again." She would be back, and next time she'd meet the people from Whitedog, too.

Stepping into the little plane, Lizzie turned at the last moment.

"Joe – are there bears here?"

"Sometimes, sure. Why?"

Lizzie glared at Bobby, who looked closely at a small mark on the window and did his best to demonstrate he hadn't heard the exchange.

As they soared above the lake, the Piper's ancient engine screaming and screeching into the sky, Lizzie looked at the waving hands, the boats lined up along the shore, and the rooftops of the cabins at Ball Lake Lodge nestled into the safety of the trees. And as they headed towards the border, she saw the logging roads, deep scars leading to vast areas where the trees were reduced to stumps and the purple fireweed claimed new territories. Silver flashes marked the courses of streams, winding their way between the trees and towards the rivers and lakes.

Barney had always instructed his pilots to stay

away from those logging roads, to show the guests instead a pristine wilderness as they flew into the lodge. Now, it would be almost impossible to do that.

In the distance, the town of Kenora looked so perfect from above with its sweep of promenade and busy streets and pontoons stretched into the lake, waiting for families to return from a day on the water.

So much was hidden in the scenes she saw. So much she still didn't know. So much she needed to learn, and so much she needed to do.

"I'll help, you know," said Lizzie's father.

Lizzie looked at him. He seemed younger somehow. The last few days had been full of seriousness and importance, but they'd also been filled with more laughter and happiness than she'd shared with her father for years. The lines had eased away from his forehead, thrown into the lake along with her and Bobby as he'd lifted them high and launched them, shrieking and squealing, into the sparkling waters.

"It's okay, Dad. I know it's Mum's family really."

"Ours. Our family, Busy Lizzie."

She settled back to watch the plane's shadow racing across the treetops, a shifting marker on the world that sent out only a fleeting message that it had ever been there at all.

CHAPTER 20

IN THE END, A NEW BEGINNING

September 15th, 2021

"And that," said Lizzie finally, "is just the beginning of the story really. Because what my great-grandfather and great-grandmother started still hasn't been finished. Barney and Marion fought with everything they had, but they ran out of time. So, you see," she jutted her chin proudly, "that's where I come in. Where, I hope, we all come in."

She shuffled her feet a little, her palms sweaty. She pushed herself to breathe slowly and evenly.

"I think what we need to remember is something really simple. The people at Grassy Narrows? All the indigenous people? They were there first."

She dared to look up to repeat the last line, slowly and firmly.

"They were there first."

Lizzie looked across at Bobby and over to her classmates and saw that the number had grown. The sky was a deep velvet blue fringed with red, the first pinpricks of stars showing bright, and all around her were people. Children from other classes. Teachers. Parents. Aunts who had been sent to pick up nieces; the school bus driver who suddenly had no children to drive and had gone in search of them.

Across to the far side of the field, people were standing and looking at her. There was a stillness for a while after she had finished speaking, and then Miss Andrews started to clap. Others joined her, clapping their hands and stamping their feet, Bobby whooping and hollering and cheering her on as loudly as his lungs would let him. As Miss Andrews applauded she tried to catch Lizzie's father's eye but she needn't have bothered: her wide smiles and coy glances were an irrelevant sideshow, caught up as he was in the girl who stood front and center.

Lizzie saw Mr. and Mrs. Bingle standing together, a vast antique baby buggy with shining wheels and a white hood that had cradled generations of Bingles before stood proudly in front of them. Inside, she knew, was their little girl, Bobby's baby sister who gurgled and slept her way through the days. Lizzie and Bobby both adored her and had spent hours carrying her around the farm, lining her up on blankets beneath different trees so the shadows danced across her face in the breeze. The wide-eyed girl could see a rainbow of colors as the leaves started to turn with the season and they fluttered, twisting and spiraling, gently settling down onto her blankets.

"Time," Mrs. Bingle had decided. "She's called Time. Because time is the most precious thing each of us has in all the world."

And Lizzie's father looked on, too. He looked at the girl who had lived in his house for so many years and who he had barely known until a few weeks ago. He saw someone with fire and strength who could hold the world in the palm of her hand. He thought about Irene Ward, about how the jurors had looked at the woman and hated her for a single defining moment in her life and how he changed that over the weeks of the trial.

It may feel as though a single moment alters everything but it was always there, waiting to happen, created by the thousand single moments that came before.

Lizzie looked back to where this had started, back

to the steps in the warm evening sun when her father had told her that the 'beginning is the moment before it all goes wrong.' And she smiled to think that he had been both right and wrong in what he'd said.

This, she knew as she looked at the crowd, was a beginning of a very different kind. This was a beginning made out of something else altogether. In his job, her father had to deal with defined endings – where people had done something so awful that there could be nothing beyond. But as long as the people of Grassy Narrows and Whitedog were fighting for a new ending, she would join and fight with them. New energy would help and she and Bobby and everybody else here could give that. It was funny to think how, just a few months ago, she had wanted to keep the story all to herself. Now, it belonged to everyone.

Lizzie didn't know it, but Miss Andrews' mind was already racing with plans for presentations and investigations, the usual corridor displays about the American Civil War and the Arrival Of The May-flower were already being mentally replaced by posters about Lizzie and Bobby's adventure, the traditions and rituals of the Ojibwe, and ways to change the future.

Lizzie couldn't wait to get started. She longed to

pack up everything in the barn and bring it to the school, to share everything they'd found. Her fingers itched to write the letters she wanted to write. She wanted to tell the story of Ball Lake Lodge to everyone: people in the small towns with their little strawberry-and-gossip-swapping lives, and people in the cities who rushed and raced and closed their ears to the clamor and the chaos around them. Lizzie knew – she just *knew* – that if enough people stood up and joined her and Bobby at the front of marches and on the covers of newspapers and on every television channel around the world, that something would have to be done. That much love and hope and caring couldn't go unnoticed.

She knew that her new friends at Grassy Narrows would once again be able to live as they wanted. The promises of the past would be pieced back together again.

And she knew she wouldn't stop until they too could say that, yes, it had been done: the world was a safe place once more.

Once, a little frog went to a race. He was very small,

and others shouted, 'You're too small, you can't race!' but he raced anyway. And along the way, he passed some of the bigger frogs who stopped to catch their breath. Others kept shouting, 'You'll never make it, you're too small!' He won the race, and they all wondered how he'd done it, especially with everyone telling him all the while he was too small and he couldn't do it.

And they didn't know the little frog was deaf, so he couldn't hear others saying the race was impossible.

I guess you'd like to know
which bits are true?

Now that you've read the book, you're probably wondering which parts really happened. I can tell you that anything about Barney and Marion Lamm is absolutely true, as is anything about the mercury tragedy. Any facts and figures you've come across are true; any stories about Barney are true (yes, even the completely mad ones), and all those comments about Marion and how she kept a close eye on everything? They're all true, too.

I learned long ago to never make the mistake of believing I was the most interesting person in the room, and without that decision to stay largely silent I may never have been told this story. I might never have heard of Barney and Marion if their daughter, Rochelle, hadn't talked to me about them.

It wasn't difficult to get drawn in. From the moment I read that Barney wanted to take guests up to the North Pole in his little plane and serve them afternoon tea, I was hooked. The more stories I heard and the more I investigated, the more fascinated I became.

Rochelle helped create this book. She grew up watching her parents and the people of Grassy Narrows and Whitedog run Ball Lake Lodge. By sharing the family's files, she made *Silver River Shadow* possible. It is Rochelle's determination to bring to light the tragedy that happened – that is still happening – in the heart of Canada that has brought this book to you.

The reality is that thousands of lives have been changed, irreversibly. No amount of money can put that right. But by telling the story and sharing the awful truth, you can help ensure it never happens again. People shouldn't be allowed to lie and get away with it. People should be made to take responsibility for their actions.

Joe and Anong don't deserve to grow up in a broken, misunderstood community. Nobody does.

As for Lizzie and Bobby? They're as real as you want them to be. I know they're out there, having adventures – and nagging her dad to take them up in the Piper. In the future there will be more secrets for them to uncover, more places to be explored, and more stories to tell.

Acknowledgements

When writing about a community that isn't your own, it's important that members of that community become part of the process. It is thanks to Rochelle's continuing close connections that we were able to speak with people from Grassy Narrows and the Ojibway community, ensuring that *Silver River Shadow* is an accurate and fair portrayal of their lives both before and after the mercury tragedy.

Tom Favell grew up in the beautiful North Woods river chain, an area so full of fish and game that for centuries it sustained many native Ojibway communities and their traditional way of life; he worked at Ball Lake Lodge for seven summers. From 2001 to 2004, he served as Chief of the Wabigoon Lake Ojibway Nation. Tom has dedicated much of his adult life to the preservation of the traditions, culture and language of the First Nation Ojibway of Northeastern

Ontario, Canada. He gave careful and considered feedback on both the illustrations and the writing, ensuring that the language and terminology were appropriate and authentic. Tom especially appreciated how the language, customs and traditions of the Ojibway were incorporated into a story that showed the unique, special relationship between the people of Grassy Narrows and Barney and Marion Lamm.

Shoon Keewatin, son of Andy Keewatin who was the Chief of the Grassy Narrows Band during the mercury crisis, also helped with the review of *Silver River Shadow*. Andy worked at Ball Lake Lodge for more than 25 years and traveled to Minamata in Japan along with Barney Lamm in order to better understand the unfolding crisis. He dedicated much time to discussions with the Ontario government along with the Dryden Chemical Company and their parent company Reed Paper Group, looking to get appropriate payouts to the community. Shoon particularly enjoyed the adventure of the story, adding that the descriptions of the lodge triggered happy memories of how life was pre-mercury.

Finally, our thanks go to Lorna Brown. Lorna lived in Grassy Narrows for 25 years, working for ten years with Health Canada to study the impact of mercury poisoning on the young people of the community, and spending a further ten years in the high school where, after some years teaching, she became the Director of Education. Lorna noted how the book skillfully, sensitively and accurately wove together historical events to create an exciting adventure story.

It is because of these people who took the time to read and consider *Silver River Shadow* that we are able to bring this book to the world. The communities of Grassy Narrows and Whitedog have been forever changed by the mercury tragedy and it has been a privilege to share their story with you.

www.jane-thomas.co.uk